THOUSAND OAKS LIBRARY

P9-CFP-979

JUL   2010

DISCARD

COLLECTION MANAGEMENT

6/14	X-2	/

THOUSAND OAKS LIBRARY
1401 E. Janss Road
Thousand Oaks, CA 91362

Between Us Baxters

To my dad and mom, Allan and Beth Hegedus,
for loving and embracing me for me. I love you.

Between Us Baxters

Bethany Hegedus

Copyright © by Bethany Hegedus
This book or parts thereof may not be reproduced in
any form, stored in a retrieval system or transmitted
in any form by any means—electronic, mechanical,
photocopy, recording or otherwise—
without prior written permission of the
publisher, except as provided by the
United States of America copyright law.

Published by WestSide Books
60 Industrial Road
Lodi, NJ 07644
973-458-0485
Fax: 973-458-5289

Library of Congress Control Number: 2008911813

International Standard Book Number: 978-1-934813-02-7
Cover illustration Copyright © by Lori McElrath-Eslick
Cover design by David Lemanowicz
Interior design by Paul Sikar

Printed in the United States of America
10 9 8 7 6 5 4 3 2 1

First Edition

j Fic
(West.)

Between Us Baxters

ONE
Meemaw and Moses

Like Moses, Meemaw had ten commandments. On Sundays, I was bound as if by the Bible to a long list of rules. Before dinner, be seen and not heard. Once at the table, lay my napkin in my lap. Keep my elbows off the table, ankles crossed. Bow my head while Uncle Jimmy presides over the prayer. Pass the rolls to my right. Don't talk with my mouth full. Use the soupspoon only for soup. Wipe my mouth with a napkin, not the back of my hand. And never leave the table before being excused.

Why, if Moses had a number eleven, Lord help me Jesus, Meemaw could have come up with another one. But Holcolm County, Georgia, beat her to it. Here we were all supposed to live by the "no befriending Negroes" rule.

Mama and I preferred to break a few commandments every now and again. And today we weren't giving credence to the one unwritten law the entire South, not just Georgia, subscribed to. This morning, we were breaking bread with the Biggses.

"Can't pick your family," Mama told me early on, "but you can pick your friends." Mama picked Henrietta Biggs—Henri for short. And I picked Timbre Ann, Henri's niece. Didn't matter to Mama and me that they were colored. Friends were friends.

"Polly, you measure the flour and I'll crack the eggs," Timbre Ann said. She headed toward the Frigidaire.

"Sure thing." I didn't bat an eye at Timbre Ann's bold, bossy self. Today wasn't just any breakfast. It was a birthday breakfast in honor of Henri's fiftieth. It had to be perfect.

I yanked on the pull cord in Judge Anderson's pantry. Too bad we couldn't have Henri's party at our place, or at the Biggses'. We had to settle for the Judge's house, where Mama worked as a nursemaid tending to the Judge's ailing mother, Old Lady Lily. And it's where Mama got Henri hired on as the Andersons' cook after Meemaw fired her. If no eyes looked in on us, the Judge's place was the safest place to celebrate. It'd more than suffice.

I scanned the shelves. Mama and I had bought the breakfast fixings earlier in the week. We hid the groceries amid the boxes, cans, and other provisions throughout the Andersons' overstocked kitchen.

I found what I was looking for. Our full flour bag. My hands shook carrying it to the counter. This party we were having was on the sly—neither the Judge nor Daddy knew we were celebrating.

"How's it coming?" Timbre Ann asked, while she poured the buttermilk.

"Good." I dumped a second cup of flour in the mixing bowl. A plume of floury smoke tickled my nose. Timbre Ann sneezed, then batted at the air.

"Careful, I'm not a ghost like you," she said, teasing.

"Is that so?" Lightning quick, I dipped my finger in the bowl and went after her. I swiped at Timbre Ann's chin. I got her.

"Polly! You're dead." She took a fistful of flour and threw it at me. It spread in a thousand different directions, like fireworks on the Fourth of July, only there was no kaleidoscope of colors. No red. No blue. There was only white.

I hadn't yet changed into my church clothes—Daddy wouldn't be here to pick us up until shortly before noon when the Judge returned—so I grabbed a fistful of that flour. I chased Timbre Ann. She screeched, laughing and screaming, trying to keep away from me. I was about to dump the flour down the neck of her blouse when Mama grabbed me by mine.

"I leave the two of you alone for five minutes and here you are, waking the dead." Mama let me go and dusted her hands together like they were the ones that were covered with powder. "Now, clean up this mess before

Miss Lily tells the Judge I let you act the fool. You want to get me fired?"

"No, ma'am," I said.

"Sorry, Miss Lisbeth," said Timbre Ann. "We got carried away."

"Apology accepted," Mama said, all gruff.

We knew not to push it. Mama meant business. I grabbed the dustpan and swept the floor. Timbre Ann did her part, too. She used a dry cloth, getting up all the excess flour before she wiped the counter.

Mama took a seat at the Judge's oak table and clipped coupons from the Sunday circular. Not for him. For us. Despite being related to Moneybags Meemaw, we Baxters were on a budget.

"You best hurry or breakfast won't be done when Henri and Sam get here," she said. Mama laid down the scissors and rubbed her forehead. Something more was on her mind than Henri's arrival.

I bit my lip. It had to be Daddy. I'd heard them late last night. Mama raised her voice. "Oh, Otis, how could you?" Daddy hushed her. "You want to wake Polly? She'll learn about it soon enough." Mama got quiet. Daddy, too. I reckoned they gave each other the silent treatment; I didn't hear another peep. For the rest of the night, I slept fitfully, worried something bitter brewed between them. If

Daddy got here before breakfast was over, it would only make things worse. I stirred the batter double-time.

Timbre Ann heated the griddle. Though I wanted to do it, I let her. At fourteen, she had two years on me. I watched as she took a forkful of butter and made figure-eights up and down the length of the pan. It sizzled, causing the butter to bubble and pop.

"Let's take turns with the batter," I said, squeezing in next to her.

"All right. Fine by me." Timbre Ann backed away from the stove, but added, "Make them silver-dollar size. Aunt Henri likes them that way."

I preferred mine as big as the plate, but I aimed to please. Soon, the smell of the cinnamon and apples that we'd added special to the mix filled the kitchen.

"Uh-hum, what's going on in here," Henri said. She snuck through the back door in her Sunday best, white gloves and all. Her pocketbook dangled at her elbow as she began unpinning her hat. "Did the Judge up and replace me with my niece while I wasn't looking?"

Timbre Ann didn't answer with a "No, ma'am." She eyed her pa, Sam, as he followed Henri through the back door. Then, she looked at Mama and me. We counted to three in our heads like we planned, and sing-said it all together: "Happy birthday!"

We circled around Henri, all talking and jabbering at once. Mama swooped in for a hug and stood on her tiptoes to kiss Henri on the cheek. Henri was solid, like a tree, and near in height to Sam, her ten-years-younger baby brother, who was patting her on the back. I settled for snagging her around the middle and burying my head in the folds of her midnight purple dress, up under her bosom. Timbre Ann stuck to her other hip.

Once the hugging was done, I announced, "Now, no lifting a finger. This breakfast is a present from me and Mama."

"And me," chirped Timbre Ann. "But I also have something special for you at home."

"My, my," said Henri. "If this is what fifty years gets you, I'll take it."

Mama took Henri to the side and presented her with her homemade birthday card. Like every year, Henri got all teary eyed. Mama called them salt-and-pepper friends, but I always thought they acted more like mother and daughter. Henri doted on Mama, and Mama did just about anything to make Henri happy. Timbre Ann watched them, too. Was she seeing us as old ladies, the same way I was?

Maybe not. Timbre Ann hadn't told me she'd gotten Henri anything. I so wanted to buy Henri this bluebird brooch, the kind I'd seen fancy ladies wear, but there was no way, no how I could scrounge enough to get it. Timbre Ann told me not to fret. Henri wasn't one to wear jewelry. Still, my longing to see that brooch pinned on Henri's chest made mine ache a little.

"Here, have a seat." I walked Henri to the head of the table and draped a fancy napkin in her lap.

We couldn't eat in the dining room. That just wasn't done. We were pushing our luck as it was, should someone see us eating around Judge Anderson's kitchen table. If we got caught, we'd have to pretend Henri was serving us. Mama and me. The thought of that made my palms itch.

"Y'all got me good," Henri said, surveying the kitchen where she was normally the one at the stove. She turned to Sam. "Here I thought Timbre Ann was traveling to compete in one of those speech contests her teacher is always entering her in."

Sam presented Henri with her fresh-squeezed orange juice. "We figured a tiny little lie wouldn't hurt."

"Any kind of fibbing hurts. Don't you go razzing me again," Henri said. She blinked, pretending to keep back a rush of fake tears. "I was starting to think y'all had forgotten about me."

"Oh, Aunt Henri," Timbre Ann said. She must've taken Henri for real. Timbre Ann left the griddle and crawled in Henri's lap like she was an itty-bitty thing. "We couldn't forget your birthday. Not for one minute."

"Never. Ever," I said, lowering the heat on the griddle.

"That's right," Mama said. "You're too important—the glue that holds us all together."

Over by the sink, the kitchen curtains fluttered. I glanced out the window. The tops of the pines waved in the wind. Good. No sign of Daddy. No sign of any breathing thing but the birds. Still, it wouldn't do to dally.

A few minutes later, I slid the pancakes, all a crisp and buttery brown, onto a platter. Mama had cooked the bacon when we first arrived. It waited piled on a plate in the stove to stay warm. I grabbed that, too, and set everything on the table, including the syrup. While we'd been chatting and cooking, Mama had cleared away the Sunday circular and had set five places. We slid into our seats.

"What did I do to deserve this?" Henri asked, shaking her head softly from side to side.

"Hush, you've been taking care of us for years—we only get one day to take care of you," Mama said. "You deserve this and more."

"You sure do," I said, thinking how fine Henri'd look wearing that bluebird brooch. *If only . . .*

Sam stopped my shopping thoughts. "Prayer time," he said, holding out his hand. Mama placed her palm in his. Henri's, too. Around and around we went—fingers finding fingers.

"Heavenly Father, we thank you for Miss Henrietta Biggs, today's birthday blessing. She is a Sister in Spirit, as well as in body. May she know how she is loved."

Sam paused and one by one, we raised our heads. A flicker of red caught my eye. Was it Daddy? The Judge? Nope, just a cardinal. It darted off a branch and flew away. Its wings flamed against the cloudless sky.

Together, we all said, "Amen."

TWO
Everyday Miracle

Despite our birthday breakfast, this Sunday was no different from any other. We were expected at Pine Bluff, Mama's childhood home, at three o'clock sharp. Normally, after services, we had to skip social time, but today Reverend Douglas's Everyday Miracles sermon ended a might early. We had time to kill.

"Polly, run and get some punch for your daddy and me," Mama said, pushing me off in the direction of the refreshment table.

"But, Mama," I said, seeing Sally Jean Taylor and her sidekick, Beverly Jenkins, in charge of doling out drinks. Three weeks into the school year I had managed to keep them both from razzing me. How? I did it by going nowhere near them.

"No buts," Mama said. "Go on, now."

"But—"

"You heard your mama, Polly-gal." Daddy used his special name for me, but his tone was sharp.

"Yessir."

As soon as I was on my way, Mama nudged Daddy. He wasn't one for social time. Not at Trinity Baptist or anywhere else, save for his weekly poker game.

"Punch, Polly?" Sally Jean asked. She and Beverly had set up under the maples.

"Three, please," I said. I glanced over my shoulder. Mama and Daddy disappeared. I didn't spot them by the edge of the parking lot where Daddy would be most comfortable. Where were they?

Sally Jean lined up a half dozen Dixie cups in front of her. "Nice dress," she said.

"Thanks." I smoothed the cotton pleats. It wasn't often I got a compliment, especially from the two of them.

The birds chittered above. Brown Thrashers—otherwise known as Ferruginous Thrush. Timbre Ann taught me that. There was nothing she didn't know.

"Eww, bird poo." Beverly pointed to a wet clumpy white streak on the bark of the maple.

"Be careful, Polly. You wouldn't want those birds to mess on your dress," Sally Jean said, handing me a paper cup.

Had she spit in there when I wasn't looking? That's just the kind of thing Sally Jean would do. I had just about decided it was safe to take a sip when she asked, "Where is it your mother shops? Colored Castoffs?"

"Or Timbre Ann's Closet?" Beverly snickered.

Tarnation. Mama hadn't bought this dress. It came from the Biggses. Another hand-me-down.

"Oh, this isn't Timbre Ann's," I said, keeping my back straight and my arms pinned to my sides. "This was a gift from my Meemaw. She also gave me a television set." That part wasn't a lie. It was an old model with a bent antenna. Meemaw had Henri wrap it up real pretty for my twelfth birthday.

"*You* have a television set," Beverly said, impressed.

"Television set or not, I know for a fact *that* dress belonged to a colored," Sally Jean said. "I was shopping for school clothes when that Timbre Ann waltzed right into Caroline's Creations. Miss Caroline tried to get rid of her, making her wait until the store was almost empty, but that Timbre Ann stood around like she had all day. If you think that beats all, why, when Miss Caroline did ring her up, she paid with a twenty-dollar bill."

A twenty-dollar bill, Lordy Lou. How much money did the Biggses have?

"Miss Caroline didn't want cooties, so she slid on her Sunday gloves. You should have seen that Timbre Ann's chin wobble. Big baby."

Surefire, I wanted to string Sally Jean up for talking about Timbre Ann that way. But I couldn't do a thing, and she knew it. Her father was Daddy's foreman at the mill.

"Sheriff Wilkes was watching. Out on the sidewalk," Beverly said. "Told her if she knew what was good for her, she wouldn't go parading around in that dress."

No wonder Mama had fooled me. This dress looked brand new because it was. Timbre Ann had never worn it.

I backed away. I didn't need Sally Jean's stupid punch and cookies.

"I better not ruin my appetite," I said, doing my best to not let her know she got to me. "I'm expected at Pine Bluff for Sunday dinner."

"Only decent meal you Baxters get is on Sunday. I'm surprised Reverend Douglas hasn't taken up an offering in your name."

Sunday or not, Sally Jean would be sipping her supper through a straw. I snapped back, ready to give her the biggest fat lip in the history of Holcolm County when Beverly screeched.

"Eww!"

That thrasher may have missed me, but Sally Jean's bangs got doused with a big white glob. Bull's eye! Bird poo dripped from her hair onto her gingham green sundress.

"Heavens!" Sally Jean screamed. "Polly Baxter, look at what you did."

Reverend Douglas and the rest of the congregation

came running. I didn't defend myself. Why should I? Sally Jean getting hit, and not me, was nothing short of an everyday miracle. The kind the Reverend spent all afternoon preaching about.

Sally Jean fretted, using her pointer fingers to try to keep the strands with the bird poo from spreading onto the rest of her curls. Her mother, Mrs. Taylor, dug in her pocketbook for a hanky, muttering "That girl" all the while.

"I understand you're upset, Sister Taylor," Reverend Douglas said. "But Polly, here, had nothing to do with this calamity. Nature does have a way of taking its course—even when we least expect it."

Everyone had a good chuckle over that—everyone but the Taylors. Mr. Taylor furrowed his brow. After the crowd dispersed, he stormed over to Daddy, who looked right pleased Sally Jean got hit by that thrasher. I couldn't help but feel he was proud of me, though I had nothing to do with it. Even the Reverend said so.

"Go wait over there," Mama said, pushing me off and then marching over to where Mr. Taylor stood chewing out Daddy.

I leaned against our rusty truck, crossing and uncrossing my arms, trying to cover my hand-me-down dress. All eyes were on us Baxters. On me, on Mama, and especially on Daddy, who was red faced, taking Mr. Taylor's tongue-lashing.

"Dammit," Daddy muttered, as Mr. Taylor stomped off. Poor Daddy. He kicked at the mound of dirt he and his boss had been standing on.

I ran over to him and slung my arms around his middle. "I can apologize. I didn't mean to get you in trouble."

Walking with me still wrapped around his middle, he patted my head and ruffled my hair. "Ain't your fault, Polly-gal," he said.

Mama shot Daddy a "tell your daughter the truth" look, but she kept her lips clamped tight. I reckoned she didn't want to draw any more attention to us than we'd already had. A few stragglers from the congregation still stood around, praising Jesus and staring our way, as if they were documenting our doings for the Almighty himself. I didn't have to ask myself what Jesus would do—I knew. I stuck out my chin and held it Timbre Ann high.

THREE
Best Behavior

My chin wobbled some. I told myself not to worry. During her time of trial, Timbre Ann's had wobbled, too.

"Go on. Get in." Mama ushered me into the truck cab. Why was she making me sit in the middle? That was her special spot. "All we need now is to be late to Pine Bluff."

On the other side of me, Daddy climbed in behind the wheel. He still hadn't shaken off his run-in with Mr. Taylor, and he drove like a demon. The pharmacy's, dime store's, and record shop's awnings blurred together in one long green streak as we raced down Magnolia Lane, named for the flower that Holcolm County, if not all of Georgia, was famous for. With Daddy driving the way he was, we reached the turnoff for Pine Bluff right quick.

The truck lurched up Meemaw's winding drive. The bumps and sharp turns, coupled with having to remember which fork to use at the table, never failed to make my stomach queasy. I hummed the hymn from church, "Victory in Jesus," hoping it would settle the pancakes I'd eaten that morning. They itched to make a reverse trip and might ruin my hand-me-down Sunday best.

"Calm yourself, Polly," Mama said, smoothing her skirt.

I did the same, though I felt like crinkling mine into a ball and pitching it out the window. She should have told me this dress came from Timbre Ann. At least then I would've been prepared for snotty Sally Jean.

Finally, we came to the end of the steep drive. Meemaw's three-story with the green shutters and trim stood stately, half-hidden by the giant elms. Up close, the mildew from the Georgia heat and humidity crept up its planks. Soon it would need a whitewash.

"Lookie here. Jimmy's done hit the jackpot." Daddy parked our falling-down Ford next to Uncle Jimmy's spanking new Buick LeSabre. The sun glinted off its candy-apple red fins, nearly blinding me.

"Best behavior," Mama said.

Was the reminder for me or Daddy? She was angry as all get out with us both.

As we slid from the cab, Uncle Jimmy called, "Check out the new car. Business is booming. Zeniths are flying off the shelves. Otis, want to take a ride? She sure is something."

"I'll pass." Daddy stuck his hands in his pockets—to keep from socking braggart Uncle Jimmy, I'd bet.

"Hard work is rewarded with monetary means," Meemaw said, not looking up from her crossword puzzle. She sounded like the voice of God, speaking from her rocker on high. I could just see it. All she needed was a rod to pound on the porch and the storm clouds would gather, thunder would rumble, and when the rains came, Daddy would be purified from whatever lazy, no-good ways Meemaw was commenting on.

Daddy knew it, too. He paraded past Meemaw and Uncle Jimmy and straight on into the house, leaving a hushed silence in his wake.

I had to do something quick. "You look might' nice today," I told Meemaw. I planted a kiss on her sandpaper cheek, hoping that would do the trick and make up for Daddy's surly manners. She reeked of whiskey.

An unspoken Meemaw commandment: No one shall mention her drinking.

"Heaven's, Polly, you were here only last Sunday." Meemaw grimaced.

Mama leaned in for her hello, but Meemaw put her hand up, putting a stop to the lovefest. "Enough." Her arm fat jiggled like Jell-O.

"Otis is coming back, isn't he? I thought I'd take us

out for a spin before dinner," Uncle Jimmy said, clueless as usual. Behind Uncle Jimmy's back, Meemaw touted Aunt Clara as the brains behind Uncle Jimmy's success. I reckoned she was right.

"Doubt it," Mama said, her voice sounding frayed, like a long-worn washcloth. "Mill laid him off."

Shoot. My everyday miracle was nothing more than a plague of locusts. Daddy was out of a job.

"Layoffs?" Uncle Jimmy said. "Why, one of my clerks said the mill was hiring half a dozen drivers. Couldn't they have transferred Otis?"

"Well," Mama said, shooting Uncle Jimmy a shut-your-trap look, "I wouldn't know about that."

"Lisbeth, lest you forget, I was not born yesterday." Meemaw set down her crossword puzzle and took a sip of her drink. We were all supposed to pretend there was nothing in it but cold Coca-Cola. "Your husband was fired, wasn't he?"

"Fired, laid off." Mama knitted her fingers together like she had in the truck. "Either way, he's out of a job."

"Because of me," I said. Stupid Sally Jean Taylor. Meemaw should know it was my fault Daddy got fired. Not his.

"No, not everything has to do with you, Polly," Mama said. I suppose she meant to say it sweet, but it came out sharp. Then, she whispered to me and me only, "Your father told me last night."

That explained last night's angry whispers and why Mama sent me off during social time. I bet Daddy was to kiss up to Mr. Taylor. When it didn't work, no wonder she sat me between them like a barbed-wire fence. For the umpteenth time, I wished they could be more like Ward and June Cleaver from *Leave It to Beaver.*

If the Cleavers had a problem they discussed things rational-like over a plate of chocolate chip cookies. But Mama baked badly. She burned cakes and pies. And Daddy? Daddy wasn't one to talk things over. A grunt and a good-bye was more his style.

My fault or not, Daddy would be fit to be tied if he heard Mama broadcasting his troubles.

"Lordy Lou, it's hot for September." I changed the subject. "It's so hot even the skeeters don't come out to bite."

"If that's your way of asking for a glass of sweet tea, help yourself," Meemaw said.

"But I'm not—"

Meemaw raised her brow.

No back talk. How many commandments could there be?

"Yes, ma'am."

I yanked the front door but good. It'd serve Meemaw

right if I let it slam behind me. But if I gave Meemaw heart palpitations, Mama might actually take a strap to my behind. Something she always threatened, but never did, not once.

One foot inside the dark foyer, I shivered. The parlor and dining room were frigid. Air conditioning. That's the one appliance I was glad we didn't own. I'd take a hot breeze over canned air anytime. It was late September, but the chilly temperatures wouldn't arrive for weeks.

"Is that you, Polly?" Aunt Clara called from the parlor.

"Yes, ma'am." Yuck. Aunt Clara was changing one of her towheaded twins on Meemaw's antique sofa. The very couch I wasn't allowed to sit on!

"Better find your father. He came stomping through here. Scared the boys to pieces."

I took a deep breath at the injustice of it all. A mistake. Jimmy or Johnny—I could never tell which was which—stank to high heaven.

"And, Polly, be a dear. Drop this in the laundry room." Aunt Clara handed me a stinky soiled diaper.

"Yes, ma'am," I said. That sweet tea had better do double duty. Despite the air conditioning, surefire, I needed cooling off.

After a pit stop in the laundry room, I found Daddy. He stood in the kitchen hunched over a bottle—a liquor bottle. The label read JACK DANIEL'S. Daddy had raided Meemaw's not-so-secret stash under the sink behind the cleaning supplies. More than once I'd wished Meemaw would grab the wrong bottle.

I scuffed my sandal on the floor, loud enough for him to know I was there.

Sly as he could, he tossed one back. "Tired of Battle-Ax Irma's company? Or did the glare off your uncle's car blind you?" he asked, surly.

"Neither. Just getting a glass of tea." I opened the Frigidaire. Daddy stashed the bottle in his breast pocket and tossed his denim jacket over his shoulder. "Thirsty? I can fix you one."

"Naww," he said.

Meemaw's heavy pitcher made my wrist shake. Tea sloshed over the rim and dripped onto the linoleum.

"Careful. Everything around here is antique. That pitcher. The floor. Old as dirt, like the Battle-Ax." Daddy looked out the window to the few dozen oak trees scattered across the yard. "Ask me, your mama has more than made it up to Irma. If we never had to show our faces at another Sunday dinner, it'd be too soon."

On my knees, I mopped my spill. I'd always had a

nagging feeling that Sunday dinners at Pine Bluff were to make up for something. What for, I wasn't sure, but Mama insisted we come, no matter what.

When I got up, Daddy was gone. He must've slipped outside, his new buddy, Jack Daniel's, along to keep him company.

FOUR
Common Courtesy

As we gathered around the dining room table, my insides turned flips. I'd seen Daddy drink a beer or two, listening to a baseball game on the radio, but never any whiskey. Mama wouldn't approve. She hated Meemaw's drinking more than anybody. How many had Daddy had? Was he drunk?

"Here you are, Polly-gal." Daddy held out my chair.

"Thanks, Daddy," I said. He couldn't be far gone. He wouldn't be so charming otherwise. Would he?

"And for you, Lisbeth." Daddy rounded the table and did the same for Mama.

"Why, thank you." Mama sat down and spread her napkin on her lap.

Aunt Clara stood behind her chair, clearing her throat, waiting for somebody to seat her.

"Coming down with something are you, Clara?" Uncle Jimmy asked, plopping right down.

Aunt Clara seated herself. "Why, yes, perhaps I am." She coughed again, I suppose for show. "Pass the water, please. I seem to have a frog in my throat."

I reached for it, but Daddy got to it first. He poured Aunt Clara a glass and presented it to her like he would a bouquet of flowers. She looked like she wanted to throw it in his face.

"Why, thank you," she said, thin lipped.

Mama beamed at Daddy in a way that said, *Forgiven. Possibly forgotten.* Now that Daddy'd one-upped Uncle Jimmy, all would be fine. Mama was back on the Baxter home team. Rooting *for* Daddy, instead of against him.

Their making up settled my stomach just in time for dinner. A good thing, because my nervousness gave way to a three-helpings hunger.

Eagerly, I surveyed the table. Along with each fancy place setting, salad fork, soupspoon, water goblet, and glass for tea was a whole host of food. A basket of puffy yeast rolls. A honey-baked ham the size of Uncle Jimmy's Buick. Green beans with fancy-schmancy pearlized onions instead of the crunchy fried ones I preferred. And a bowl of whipped potatoes heaped to overflowing next to a crystal gravy boat.

"Look at all this food, Mother," Mama said, in the buttery tone she reserved for seeking Meemaw's approval.

"No need to go to so much trouble every week. You should be saving your strength."

"My strength does not need saving." Meemaw raised her chin, challenging any of us to say otherwise. She nursed her drink. "Besides, it's Clara who takes on most of the work." With one breath, Meemaw blew out the candle that Daddy's gallantry had lit on Mama's face. Meemaw didn't even stop to take notice, but continued, "Since Henrietta left us in a pinch, going to work for Judge Anderson the way she did—"

"Henri was fired," I said. Leave it to Meemaw to rewrite history. Timbre Ann hadn't taken those candlesticks. Henri had every right to speak up for her niece.

"Polly, dear, I had hoped you wouldn't take after your mother here and develop lifelong friendships with the hired help." Meemaw's lips pursed. "How is Timbre Ann these days, still gangly and knock-kneed?"

How dare Meemaw talk about my best friend that way!

"All legs and teeth. Like a horse," Daddy said. And before I could chastise him, Mama did.

"Otis, she's just a girl. She's growing into her looks is all," Mama said.

"That whole family is uppity," said Uncle Jimmy. "I blame that father of hers. He's getting too big for his britches," he continued, launching into a tirade about how coloreds should stay in their place.

I balled my hand into a fist. My fingernails cut into my palm.

Mama laid her hand over mine. When Uncle Jimmy finally shut his trap, Mama swallowed deeply, careful not to let her patience be tried. "In any case, you've outdone yourself, Mother. Dinner looks delicious."

"Don't thank me," Meemaw said, mean as spit. "Clara's the one who carries me to the market. Wakes her husband and baby boys at the crack of dawn to attend the early service, all so we can dine in the manner we're accustomed to."

"I offer to do those things, Mother, but you always remind me that Clara lives closer."

"On the *right* side of town," I piped up.

Meemaw raised her brow, displeased that I had talked out of turn. "Lisbeth, you should have taken better measures to see your daughter did not inherit your jealous streak." She bowed her head. "Now, James, lead us in the blessing."

Commandment number four: Uncle Jimmy shall preside over the prayer.

"Why doesn't Daddy," I offered, unable to bite my tongue.

Before Uncle Jimmy could clasp his hands, Daddy began: "Rub a dub dub, thanks for the grub, yay God."

Meemaw's cheeks flamed. "Otis, show some respect."

Daddy spooned some green beans onto his plate. Next he speared himself a slice of ham.

"Ask me, the Lord in heaven frowns more on a mother pitting her two daughters against one another than He does a rhyme about giving thanks."

Meemaw drew herself to her feet. She rested her palms flat on the table. "You are a fine one to talk to me about pitting—"

"Mother, your blood pressure," said Aunt Clara, sitting Meemaw back in her chair. She draped the napkin over her lap and turned to Daddy. "Otis, apologize."

"No can do. I meant what I said."

Amen, my insides shouted.

Aunt Clara fanned herself with her linen napkin. "Well, I never."

"Never? Well, I suspect you did," Mama said. "Otherwise, how'd you get those twins?"

Uncle Jimmy, who'd been shoveling food into his mouth, shot out green beans on that one.

"Good one, Mama," I said. Oops. Another commandment broken—talking with my mouth full.

"Enough," Meemaw said. "I will not have Sunday

dinner made into a mockery. Lisbeth, you and *yours* should leave us to enjoy this meal."

"Oh, Mother, we were only kidding." Mama fiddled with her napkin. "We meant no harm. At our house, it's common to tease one another."

"'Common' is correct." Meemaw looked at Mama like we were tarnished old pennies. "Thank heavens your father didn't live to see exactly how *common* you've become."

Mama's eyes welled. She had loved her father something fierce. I willed her not to cry. Not to give Meemaw the satisfaction.

"We are waiting," Meemaw said.

Daddy got to his feet. "Your daughter, Lisbeth Baxter, mind you, ain't got a common bone in her body."

Gentlelike, he took Mama's arm and led her from her seat. She didn't seem to be able to walk on her own. Since her wisecrack, Mama'd frozen like a deer in headlights. Not me. I stood right quick and accidentally-on-purpose knocked over my chair as I did. The twins jumped at the noise. Johnny, no Jimmy, started wailing.

"Polly Beatrice Baxter!" Meemaw said.

Daddy and Mama had defied Meemaw with their words. I reckoned I could make a statement with my top-pled-over chair.

"Adios," I said.

Out the front door, down the porch steps, and we were free. After the chilly temperature inside, the humid air warmed my bones. We slid into the truck. Daddy gunned the engine and slammed the truck into reverse.

"Careful," Mama said, unthawing now that she was out from under Meemaw's gaze. "We wouldn't want to ding Jimmy's new Buick." The catch in her voice made it sound like a suggestion.

"Naw, we sure wouldn't," Daddy said. "Would we, Polly?"

"No, sir," I said. "That'd be common."

FIVE
Moon Pie in the Sky

Daddy hit the brakes in the nick of time. There'd be no fender bender tonight. Instead, Daddy leaned out the rolled down window, flipped open his pocketknife and "keyed" Uncle Jimmy's candy-apple car from one bumper to the other. Even before I heard that grinding sound, metal on metal, I knew we Baxters had been ousted forever from the Pritchard clan. No more Sunday dinners. Daddy messing with Uncle Jimmy's car simply sealed our fate.

"Not so shiny now," Daddy said, as Mama rocked herself back and forth.

When Meemaw didn't storm the front porch, I was sure our antics had her phoning the police. I kept watch for signs of Sheriff Wilkes in the rearview mirror. Nope. No flashing lights. No siren.

Daddy drove slowly, as if our getaway was nothing more than a Sunday drive. Mama was back in her old spot, her knees touching Daddy's as he shifted gears. I hugged the door, staring out the window, wondering why Meemaw never liked me none.

Her disapproval was nothing new. She didn't take to my chewed-up nails, my scabby knees, or my brand of dinner manners. But my being friends with Timbre Ann truly mortified her. I reckoned that was the real reason she accused Timbre Ann of taking those candlesticks. To get her out of my life and Henri out of Mama's—for good.

Meemaw's plan backfired. Three months ago, Mama got Henri hired on at Judge Anderson's, and after school Timbre Ann studied there, same as me. Unlike when we were growing up around Pine Bluff, Timbre Ann and I didn't play paper dolls anymore, but we still licked cake and cookie batter bowls and traded secrets the way boys would swap baseball cards. No way, no how, would we outgrow each other.

Halfway home we made a pit stop at Teensy's Garage and Service Station. Mama and I waited in the truck. Daddy climbed out and kept Teensy company while he pumped the gas.

When it came time to pay, Daddy followed Teensy inside the small store. On his way, he stooped to pick up a For Sale sign that had fallen. I could see him discussing it with Teensy over the soda counter while Mama knitted her knuckles together.

"Gracious sakes," Mama said, more to herself than to me. "Clara will never let us live this down." She started to come unraveled, her chest rising and falling.

"Don't worry, Mama. We're better off on our own. Honest."

"I wish that was so," she said. "I wish. I wish so many things."

Tears sprung to her eyes. I rubbed her back, hoping it would settle her. Daddy was heading back.

He neared my window. "Teensy is selling," he said. "I could make a fine living owning my own business."

"Where would we get that kind of cash?" Mama asked, grabbing an old paper napkin from the glove compartment. She wiped at her runny mascara. "Money doesn't grow on trees."

Daddy wound up his arm, stretching it out, like he was about to throw a fast pitch. "Ain't that the truth. But if I could get the funds together, imagine."

Maybe if Daddy owned his own business, we'd be rich, too. We could pull up to Uncle Jimmy's store in a new and even shinier car and pay cash money for one of those Zenith televisions. And I wouldn't have to wear Timbre Ann's hand-me-downs.

"You'd be a good businessman, Daddy."

"See, Polly believes in her old man." Daddy rounded

the truck. From the rearview mirror, I saw him sling a brown paper sack into the back of the pickup, securing it in his toolbox, so the contents wouldn't up and fly away.

"What's in there?" I asked, as he climbed back behind the wheel.

"Dinner and dessert." He turned onto Rural Route 5. "We still got to eat, don't we?"

Three tins of pork and beans later, I clanged my spoon on the front porch banister. "Best Sunday dinner I've had all year," I said, and I meant it. Meemaw could choke on her fancy-schmancy green beans for all I cared.

"Sure is, Polly-gal." Daddy bent his knees and I slid between them. Beside us, Mama watched the sunset. Its orangey pink glow erased the last traces of a too-long day. If a stranger had happened upon us, I bet we'd have looked like a true-blue television family, even if we were one child short of making the grade.

"Anyone want a Moon Pie?" I asked, ready for dessert. The day may have started out shaky, but sitting around enjoying one another like we were, it was ending mighty nice.

"Why, but of course." Mama tried to make her voice chipper, but the tears had sapped her strength.

I reached for Daddy's bag of goodies. Maybe chocolate would cheer her.

Taking the bag, Daddy said, "Let me. My treat," and doled out the Moon Pies.

While I yanked on the crinkled packaging, Daddy eased a bottle from his denim jacket. "How about a toast?"

"Where'd you get that?" Mama asked. She crossed her arms over her chest. "It's Sunday. Teensy's can't sell liquor on Sundays."

"Under the sink where the Battle-Ax keeps her booze," Daddy said. "She wouldn't miss one bottle. Not the way she goes through them."

Mama stood. She picked up her pumps from where she'd cast them aside when we sat down. I cringed, thinking she might throw them.

"Oh, Otis. You've been drinking," Mama said. "Is that why that nonsense started back there?"

"What nonsense?" Daddy scooted from behind me, shot lightning quick to his feet.

"That grace of yours. 'Rub a dub dub.' "

My eyes flitted from Daddy to Mama to Daddy. They only ever fought after I went to bed, when they thought I couldn't hear them. Had they forgotten I was sitting here?

"Oh yeah, and that was plenty worse than that comeback of yours, wasn't it? 'Otherwise how'd you get them twins?' " Daddy said. "It's not enough you stole me from Clara, you got to keep getting the better of her."

What? What was Daddy talking about? Steal him from Clara? I felt sick. Sick to my stomach.

"That was high school, Otis," Mama spat. "Maybe I should have let her have you."

Stop it, my insides shouted. Why couldn't I say it out loud? *Stop it. Stop it.*

"You promised me you'd never drink," Mama said, close to tears. "You know what it was like growing up with her."

"A couple of sips doesn't make me a drunk. It makes me a man." Daddy tossed one back, the same swift movement as in Meemaw's kitchen.

I balled my Moon Pie wrapper in my fist. I wanted to fling it at Daddy. With Meemaw, Aunt Clara, and Uncle Jimmy ganging up on us, I'd forgotten Daddy sneaking shots. And here I was thinking he saved the day: a knight with a pocket-knife.

Mama looked like she wanted to wring his neck. Instead she wrung her hands. "She kicked us out. Do you know what that means? How're we going to . . . no more . . . oh, never you mind—" She stopped, took a deep breath, holding back whatever was on the tip of her tongue. "Otis, there is nothing Mother loves more than holding something over our heads."

"You and your highfalutin' family," Daddy said. "You think they want us there any more than we want to be there? I did us all a favor."

His eyes went wild. Meaner and madder than I'd ever seen Meemaw's.

"And don't you go blaming this all on me, Lisbeth. You were full of piss and vinegar back there, too." Daddy drank a shot. His lips puckered and then with a small grunt, they broke into a grin. He poured another shot and offered it to her. "C'mon, sweetness, you should be happy. Drink with me. Toast the end of Battle-Ax Irma's reign."

Stone-faced, Mama took the glass. She swirled the liquor.

"Henri may have raised me," Mama said, watching it go round and round. "But my mother is still my mother. I won't drink to spitting in her eye."

With that, she turned that shot glass end over end. The amber-colored smelly stuff spilled onto the porch and dripped into the weeds below.

My belly didn't even have time to settle before Daddy snatched the shot glass back. "So that's how it is, huh? The Battle-Ax wins again. Just remember who planted permission seeds back there—you, not me."

"C'mon inside, Polly," Mama ordered, somehow remembering that I sat at their feet. She yanked on the screen door. "School day tomorrow."

My legs felt glued to the stairs. I sat stock-still, unable to move.

"You heard your mother. Bedtime."

I slid under Mama's arm and on into the house, without even stopping to kiss Daddy good night.

SIX
TLC

My bedroom windows faced the back of the house. I wished they faced the front. Then, at least, I would've been able to smell Daddy's cigarette smoke wafting through the window. After Mama left, I could lean up to the screen and whisper "good night" to him.

Mama smoothed back my hair and gave me a forehead kiss. "Don't worry, darling. Get some good sleep. Everything will be fine in the morning."

I bit my lip and nodded. Mama's words sounded hollow, as if they were coming out of the old tree log Timbre Ann and I had found one day in the woods. We crouched at opposite ends, our own brand of telephone. All of Holcolm had to obey, no matter what. "No one will call me hateful names again," Timbre Ann had said. "Or treat me like trash," I called out. Our words sounded hollow, too, but it didn't stop us from saying them.

Mama made her way to the door. She flicked off my light. "Sleep tight," she said.

"Don't let the bedbugs bite," I said, finishing off our nightly routine.

Mama closed my door. She'd washed up when I did, and I listened as the floorboards creaked as she made her way to her room. She didn't say good night to Daddy, or call him in from the front porch, either. I reckoned she had a right to be mad.

She once told me that if I ever started drinking, she'd take a strap to my behind, no matter how big I got. "The devil's drink ruins lives," she said. "And not just your own."

I sighed, my heart heavy, and pitched myself to one side, and then the other. It wasn't fumble-around-in-the-dark pitch-black in my room, not with the moonlight sneaking in through my curtains. I didn't feel like sleeping, so I snuck *The Adventures of Tom Sawyer* out from under my mattress.

I knelt by the window, hoping there would be enough light to see by. There wasn't. So I just sat there, listening to the crickets making their nighttime noise, and I watched the tree branches swaying in the wind. There was a nest — a robin's nest — that I'd had my eye on for weeks. I'd never take it out of the elm it was nestled in, but if ever it fell, I'd add it to my collection.

Collections were all the rage. Stamps. Comic books. Bottle caps. Birds' nests sounded funny compared to those things, but I didn't care. A collection was for its owner, no one else—and anyways, a ton of tender love and care went into building them. They were a thing of beauty. Birds of all types looked for just the right twigs, pine straw, and dry grass to needle together and make a comfy home. Imagine that. All that love being laced into something before the babies were even born.

I'd been longing for this fancy display case I saw in the Woolworth's store window. Another purchase, along with that bluebird brooch, I'd never make. So I made do as best I could. I lined the bottom drawer of my dresser with my now raggedy baby blanket and one of Daddy's denim shirts. That way my nests wouldn't break if jostled.

"God and Mother Nature work in cahoots," Henri was fond of saying. "When one deals you a blow, the other is always there."

I didn't feel like saying a prayer so I went and got my favorite nest and sat with it back by the window. It was tiny. So tiny.

The day I found it, I had been playing hide-and-seek at Timbre Ann's. We were keeping busy while Mama and Henri put the finishing touches on a coconut cake—Timbre Ann's birthday cake.

"Ninety-eight, ninety-nine, one hundred," Timbre Ann called. "Ready or not, here I come!"

With no time left, I dove underneath the Biggses' back porch. Timbre Ann was sure to find me there, but I'd dillydallied too long, ruling out every other good hiding spot I saw. I had no choice.

And there it was, so close to my behind that one of the stray twigs poked me in the butt.

"Oww." I brushed it away, thinking I almost sat on one of Sam's whittling tools. Out it tumbled into a patch of sunlight. An itty-bitty nest.

"Come out, come out wherever you are!" Timbre Ann called. I could hear her getting closer, her footsteps pounding the dry dirt.

Something told me if Timbre Ann caught me with that nest, she'd make me fork it over. So as gentle as I could, I snuck it into my skirt pocket.

"Gotcha," she said a moment later, not noticing the bulge. She had no clue about me taking her nest. She still didn't.

I climbed in bed and made a curved resting place in my pillow. I laid Timbre Ann's nest in it. Her mama had died giving birth to her, but Sam and Henri had made sure Timbre Ann got everything that baby bird did. And me? I couldn't help but want some of that TLC—just for me.

SEVEN

Daughterly Duty

The next morning I awoke to too-bright sunshine fil-tering through my bedroom curtains. Curtains Mama and I had pieced together last spring from a checkerboard tablecloth. Mama'd said the red and white checks would be a good reminder to greet each day like a picnic. All too soon I remembered that today would be no picnic. Not after last night.

Battle lines had been drawn between the Pritchards and us Baxters, and then again between Mama and Daddy. It reminded me of the warning Henri would give when Timbre Ann and I neared the train tracks that separated the colored section of town from Chessup Street, where we lived. "Be wary at the crossroads," Henri would say. "Some you can't cross back over."

Maybe Henri hadn't been talking about trains at all, but all kinds of things you couldn't take back. Like ruin-ing Uncle Jimmy's new Buick with a pocketknife, for one. Stealing your sister's boyfriend, for another.

Surefire, Daddy'd been some big baseball hero back in his day, but date Aunt Clara? Goodness me. I bolted upright. If Mama hadn't stolen Daddy, could Aunt Clara have ended up my mama? The very idea gave me the shivers.

Mama rapped on my bedroom door. "Hurry and hustle," she said. My Monday-morning reminder. Seven-thirty on the dot.

"Yes, ma'am," I said. Ha! I was wrong to worry. Mama sounded her same old self again. I bet Daddy was in the kitchen, singing along to the tunes on WKTO, ready to get a jump on his job hunting.

I tossed on one of Timbre Ann's old dresses, the mustard yellow one, and wished for the umpteenth time that Mama's sewing skills could handle a dress pattern. As much as I liked my curtains, I'd gladly have traded them for a homemade dress where I was the one and only owner. Sally Jean's ribbing meant to make me ashamed. And it did. Not because I was friends with a colored girl, but because her daddy, not mine, could afford store-bought dresses.

One foot out of my bedroom, I stopped cold. Our pillbox house was right small; I didn't need to so much as squint to make out the empty Jack Daniel's bottle, halfhidden, in a cotton sheet on the sagging sofa. No need to be one of Hoover's FBI men to figure out Daddy had slept there, not where he belonged, across the hall from me, in bed with Mama.

I forced myself to keep moving. Straight to the kitchen. No WKTO. No singing. Mama and Daddy bristled by each other, saying nary a word.

"Scrambled this morning," said Mama. "No time for hardboiled." She jab-jab-jabbed at the eggs with her spatula. I wondered if by the time she got done cooking them, they'd be edible at all.

Daddy's eyes were red. Bloodshot, like I'd seen Meemaw's look from time to time. He poured me a glass of milk and set the percolator on to brew. He stopped to kiss me on top of the head. I reckoned that was his way of saying "Morning, Polly-gal," without uttering a single syllable. Fine. I wouldn't talk to him, neither.

I sidled up to the table, pretending the prickly-porcupine quiet didn't bother me none. I dug out my English notebook. I'd use the quiet time to memorize *impartial*, one of this week's vocabulary words. As long as I said I did my best, Mama and Daddy wouldn't care if I missed half the list, but Timbre Ann would be disappointed with anything less than a 100 percent on tomorrow's test.

Ever since she graduated top of her seventh-grade class two years ago, Timbre Ann had some fool notion I'd get the same honor when I finished primary school this

June. My brains were nowhere near as big as Timbre Ann's. I reckoned she suspected as much but wanted the honor bestowed upon me for the pure satisfaction of seeing my picture in the *Holcolm Sentinel*. They never did run hers. Despite *Brown v. the Board of Education*, desegregation had not spread to Holcolm County. And if the Citizens Council had their way, as Uncle Jimmy said, there would be no "integrating," "race mixing," or "mongrelization" in Holcolm anytime soon.

To make up for the slight, Sam plastered Timbre Ann's picture on the handheld church fans he sponsored under an advertisement for his shop's services. Her pearly whites loomed large under the slogan, DON'T DESPAIR, CALL BIGGS REPAIR. All summer long, the members of Mount Zion kept cool by waving those fans around. If you ask me, that kind of to-do was plenty better than appearing in one measly newspaper edition.

When I was done committing *impartial* to memory, as in treating or affecting all equally as defined by my dictionary, breakfast was ready.

Daddy poured himself and Mama a cup of muddy-looking coffee. Mama grimaced when she took a sip, but she drank it down without milk or sugar. She teased him almost every morning about his being so sweet he didn't need two lumps of sugar like she did, but not today.

Today, she slid the piled-high plates onto the table and then backed up against the counter to sip her coffee, as far away from Daddy as she could get.

"Thanks, Mama." One look at the overly-scrambled scrambled eggs and I knew they'd be impossible to eat with a fork. I grabbed a spoon from the silverware glass Mama kept in the center of the table.

Daddy didn't bother changing utensils. To keep the crumbly bits from falling, he propped an elbow on the table and held his plate directly under his chin. He shoveled in those eggs in record time. He ate so fast he belched.

Mama raised her brow in disgust. I could see they were in a competition to see who could stay silent the longest. Both of them acting so sandbox silly was more than I could stand. I reached for a biscuit and oops, I accidentally-on-purpose spilled my milk.

"Jesus H. Christ," Daddy said.

"Polly Beatrice Baxter," Mama said, "you've got to be more careful." She swatted at my mess with a dish towel.

Daddy backed up his chair so none would drip in his lap. I did the same, but my chair tipped back, fell over, and hit the linoleum something fierce.

See if you can keep quiet now.

Daddy got down on the floor. He cradled my head in his lap.

"Gracious, is she all right?" Mama crouched next to him, leaning on his shoulder.

"I think she'll live. Won't you, Polly-gal?"

I blinked a couple of times, pretending I had to see through a misty fog, and propped myself slowly onto my elbows. "Reckon so."

My acting job may not have been *As the World Turns* dramatic. My recovery was more *I Love Lucy* funny. It sure tickled Daddy. He howled, making Mama see red.

"Knock it off. Your daughter could have a concussion."

"Not likely." Daddy helped me to my feet. "*Our* daughter is quite the actress. Looks like we've been had."

Cat out of the bag, I bowed, low and long, almost losing my footing for real in the spilled milk.

"Adios." My daughterly duty done, I snatched my schoolbooks and lunch sack off the counter.

"Go on, get." Mama sounded mad, but I could tell she was pleased my pratfall had defrosted the ice-cube air. She caught me and swatted my behind as I slipped out the screen door. I sprinted, hoping against hope that the bridge I'd built between Mama and Daddy would hold—at least for a little while.

EIGHT
Tongue and Temper

Like a thermometer climbing, degree by degree, my day got worse as it went along. By the time I got to our willow, where I met Timbre Ann before and after school, she had already left. Her school, Washington High, was another mile farther on. Not only was she a straight-A student, she was Miss Punctuality, too.

If she would've been there, I planned on spilling my guts. Mama and Daddy might be talking, but I needed to know how to make things better, to mend things right. Timbre Ann would know how, but I'd have to wait an entire school day before I saw her.

Not long after the pledge, Miss Kilburn put up a never-ending long division problem on the chalkboard.

"Class, this is an example of what will be on the refresher test next week."

Sally Jean raised her hand. "May I move closer to the board, ma'am?" she asked. Beverly Jenkins was out sick. Lots of kids hadn't come to school today. Five out of twenty in my class alone. Miss Kilburn said if any more of us stayed out, the governor would call her in for questioning.

"Why, yes, you may." Miss Kilburn sounded like she could pin a star to Sally Jean's peaches-and-cream blouse for using *may* instead of *can*. Their teacher's-pet lovefest made me want to puke.

"Thank you, ma'am."

Sally Jean, who normally sat two seats behind me and to my right, had moved to Craig Thorton's empty desk. She picked his on purpose. She settled in beside me.

I stared at my page, trying hard to work the math problem. Normally, there was nothing I loved more than numbers. Counting them calmed me. A trick Mama had taught me, passed on from Granddaddy. Mama told me he loved numbers something fierce. I did, too—until I got to long division. Those stupid problems kicked my tail in fifth grade, and again now in seventh, when they were supposed to be easy.

"What's the trouble, Polly? Can't count that high?" Sally Jean asked.

I bent my head over my desk. If there was one thing

my hair was good for, aside from getting tangled, it was blocking folks out. Magic. Sally Jean all but disappeared.

I stared at the problem: 2,743,225 divided by 33.

I tried to break it down the way Timbre Ann showed me. I took the 33 and tried to multiply it by something that got close to the first three numbers in that jumbo problem. Five wasn't even close. I tried 7 next. Finally, I got what I guessed was the first number: 8. What was I supposed to do next? Subtract? Drop another number down?

Sally Jean muttered, "How double-A disgusting," drawing Miss Kilburn's and my attention to the droplets of blood on my scratch paper. Without knowing I'd done so, I'd chewed my fingernails to the quick.

"Heavens, go wash up," Miss Kilburn said, examining my hands. "Then come back and get a Band-Aid."

I got up, my face burning.

"Don't fault Polly, Miss Kilburn," Sally Jean said, sweet as sugar. "I bet she's hungry. My daddy fired hers for fighting on the job."

"Sally Jean." Miss Kilburn's voice issued a warning, but I barely heard. *That's why Daddy was fired? For fighting?* As I made my way down the aisle, I accidentally-on-purpose stepped on Sally Jean's saddle shoe.

"Ain't hungry at all," I said. "I bite my nails to keep from backhanding you!"

Miss Kilburn silenced the chittering class by giving the whole room—not just me—the evil eye.

"Polly, I will see you after school," Miss Kilburn said. She handed me the bathroom pass and I slunk out into the hallway. Detention.

NINE

The Weepy Willow

Timbre Ann sat under our willow. I always thought that tree—that once upon a time had been struck by lightning—was the sorriest sight. A jagged scar split its knotted, gnarled trunk. Octopus-like limbs spread every which way, drooping and sagging like willows do. Our tree truly looked like it would cry if it could.

But today, seeing Timbre Ann, her back up against the bark, hunched over her schoolbooks, our willow didn't look sad at all, but proud at providing shelter.

"Late this morning. Late now." Timbre Ann gathered her books and got to her feet. "Is everything all right?"

I had wanted to heap my family's problems on her, to have her tell me what to do to stop Mama and Daddy from fighting, but after my detention, I just couldn't.

"Jim-dandy." I set off along our regular route, leaving our willow and cutting through the woods, past the ravine, to the Andersons' back door. The day's events boiled inside me.

"Wait for me, it's quiz time," Timbre Ann said, ready to start our study session. She shuffled her books under one arm and held her palm out, waiting for me to hand over my vocabulary list.

"Can't. I spilled milk on it over breakfast and meant to, but forgot to ask Miss Kilburn for a new list."

"Forgot. How? I quiz you every day, including test day, when you get new words."

"Well, you see . . ." Despite my long strides, Timbre Ann caught up to me. No way, no how would she think my outburst was acceptable. (Neither did Miss Kilburn. She assigned me to write "I will hold my tongue and my temper" on the blackboard fifty-five times as punishment.) "Miss Kilburn, she, she got busy with other things."

There. Not the gospel truth, but not an out-and-out lie.

"Besides, I bet I ace the test. Had me plenty of study time over breakfast. I learned a new word: 'impartial.'" I recited the definition for her: treating or affecting all equally. "Should be easy. Miss Kilburn says the word aloud and we just have to jot it down with the definition. Penmanship counts."

"She should have y'all use it in a sentence. My teacher does." Timbre Ann cleared her throat and gestured to the pines as if they were her audience. "Ladies and gentlemen of the jury, in today's proceedings, it is of utmost

60

importance to be impartial. Otherwise justice cannot, will not, be served."

I clapped, forgetting to hide my bandaged fingers. Timbre Ann didn't notice. Her enacting her lawyer dreams snatched me off the hook from any explaining. "Ask me, you sound more like a lawyer than Perry Mason."

"If I study hard, keep up my elocution lessons, Miss Wrenshaw says Howard Law School may be in my future. Nothing wrong with Howard, but I plan on going to Harvard."

"Harvard?" I echoed. I didn't know much about fancy colleges, but I knew Harvard was one of the best. It was up north.

Timbre Ann stopped walking. "You've got to promise not to tell Aunt Henri. Cross your heart and hope to die?"

I made a big X over my heart. "But why?"

"She thinks Howard Law School is shooting high enough. But Pa started me a college fund." Timbre Ann hopped a fallen log and landed on the other side. "And he may have been razzing me, but he said, 'Hoity-toity Harvard ain't even good enough for my little girl.' That's how I got the idea. Harvard."

I tried to take that log in one long leap as Timbre Ann had, but my foot caught and I pitched forward.

Timbre Ann steadied me. She put her hands on my

shoulders to keep me from falling. "Careful," she said. "You got to watch where you're going if you're going to keep up with me."

She was joking. I knew she was joking, but her tone reminded me of Sally Jean, who made me feel less than, so she could be greater than, like some lopsided equation. Without warning, I wanted out of those woods. And fast.

"Ready, set, run," I said. I shot off with a heck of a head start.

"No fair," Timbre Ann yelled, taking off, too.

I pumped my legs harder. "Last one at the Andersons' is a rotten egg."

TEN
Fulbright's

Racing to the Andersons' became our new ritual. I'd meet Timbre Ann at the willow and then we'd take off running. I thought she'd put a stop to it. Tell me to knock off the nonsense, but she didn't. Our racing became serious business. As serious as quiz time used to be.

That first day, detention day, she beat me, and the next day, too. Our racing wasn't fair—she had a knapsack for her books while I had to run with mine flat up against my nonexistent chest. She won, lickety-split.

After that I got wise. I knew better than to ask Mama to get out her needle and thread to sew me a book bag. Things were only so-so at home. I hadn't spotted any signs of Daddy drinking, but he was still sleeping in the living room. The worn sheet he covered himself with wasn't stashed under the couch; it was now folded hastily and stuffed in the hallway closet so I'd be none the wiser. That's where I found it, when I scrounged up an old pillowcase to serve as a makeshift book bag.

Not that my pillowcase made us equals. I was nowhere near as tall as Timbre Ann. Daddy had said Timbre Ann was all legs and teeth, like a horse. Surefire, she ran like one.

"You ready to give up? Give in?" she asked today, as she neared the willow.

"Never!" I told her. And before we could chant, "ready, set, run," I slung my pillowcase of books over my shoulder and took off.

I got a good ways ahead when she ran up beside me, not even out of breath. "Even cheating, you can't beat me," she said, and she sprinted ahead, her side-braids bouncing on her shoulders.

"That so?"

I kicked my knees and swung my elbows, doing my best to catch up to her and not send my schoolbooks flying. My chest heaved, and my breath came out in puffs. I sounded like Old Lady Lily. Sweat began to drip off my nose, but it just made me run harder.

Soon we were neck and neck.

"Told Pa we're racing. He says it's good for me, for my lungs, for my legs, but Aunt Henri wouldn't like it. 'Child, that ain't ladylike. Sweating and fussing and carrying on.'"

Was she making fun of Henri? Who did she think she was? The Queen of Sheba?

I pumped my legs as hard as I could, aiming to teach Miss Too Big for Her Britches a lesson. I ducked under branches and hopped fallen logs like my next meal depended on me coming up the winner. I didn't once look over my shoulder. *Ha, and I did it.* First. I got to the Andersons' back door first.

Henri and Mama sat around the Judge's kitchen table. They had their heads bent together, sipping coffee despite the Indian summer heat. I slipped inside, quietly shutting the screen door. Neither noticed me; they were too busy, Henri shaking her head and holding some kind of flier.

"I don't believe it," Mama said. "This is terrible. Terrible."

Over Henri's shoulder, I made out the words: rich nigger = dead nigger. My breath caught.

Mama grabbed the crinkled sheet of paper. " 'Close your doors now,' " Mama read, not noticing me. "Who sent this?"

"Bet it was the Council, taking up Klan tactics," Timbre Ann said, coming in behind me. She let the screen door slam. No one chastised her. That flier was serious business all right. "And they didn't send it. They threw it through the shop window tied to a brick."

That couldn't be. The Citizens Council was supposed to make sure schools stayed segregated—colored or white.

The Klan, on the other hand, was all about dirty dealings. Always was. Scaring folks whatever way they knew how: lynchings, beatings, burning crosses. But if what Timbre Ann said was true, why, then both groups were cut from the same cloth, even if the Council didn't dress up in pointy hoods.

Mama hopped up from the table. Her hands lingered on Henri's shoulders. She gave her a reassuring squeeze. "Idle threats. Some folks have nothing better to do than make idle threats, but we do, don't we?" She came to me, pushed back my sweaty bangs, and smooched me on the forehead. "We've got homework to do, dinner to cook." She glanced at the ceiling, toward Old Lady Lily's room. "Sick folks to take care of. We're plenty busy. Plenty." Mama slapped the counter. "Shoot, Polly, I almost forgot. Do you think you could do Henri a favor and run to the store?"

"Sure," I said. Anything to get out of more long division. Miss Kilburn hadn't let up on us yet.

"Did the Judge make a change to the supper menu?" Timbre Ann asked. She took her schoolbooks out of her knapsack and stacked them on the table.

Henri made a *tsk* sound. "That man," she said. Judge Anderson changed his mind about the menu at least three times a week. "And my brother wonders why I never married."

Henri pulled two quarters from an envelope in the silverware drawer. Timbre Ann swiped them before Henri could hand them to me.

"I'll go," Timbre Ann said. "What is it you need?"

Mama placed her hands on her hips. "Nonsense," she said. "Miss Future Attorney at Law here has her studies to keep up. Look at that stack of books."

"I only have history. The rest are novels Miss Wrenshaw set aside for me."

Mama picked one up. "*Uncle Tom's Cabin*. Lord, I don't remember reading this."

"Books, books. The only one I care about is this one right here." Henri shoved a cookbook under Timbre Ann's nose. "Changed his mind and wants chocolate soufflé and here I made my coconut cake."

That cake sat nearby, pretty as a picture on the edge of the counter. I swiped some frosting. Sucked it off my finger. How I loved Henri's coconut cake.

"Y'all can have a piece when you get back from the store." Henri slipped a glass cover over the cake. "Get a dozen eggs, and hurry now; the Judge's guests are expected at seven."

We crossed the lawn and headed toward Judge Anderson's shed. In it were a pair of old bicycles. Timbre Ann took the red one, which left me with the blue.

Things were prickly quiet. I didn't know what to say. That flier scared me. Mama may have said it was an idle threat, but it sure sounded like someone had it out for Sam. For all the Biggses.

Timbre Ann spoke first. "Don't go getting a swelled head. I let you win," she said. But I knew she didn't. She was just saving face. Like me not telling her about Daddy drinking or us getting ousted from Meemaw's Sunday dinners.

We wheeled the bikes around the side of the house and past the columned porch, out into the street. Gripping the handlebars, I climbed on.

"Sorry. About that flier, that brick."

Timbre Ann grimaced, which made her eyebrows poke together, the way I imagine mine did when I was working a long division problem. "Thanks," she said.

"Are you scared?" I asked.

"Afraid of some namby-pamby white folk?" Timbre Ann said. "No." She tossed her leg over her bike. "C'mon, we better go. Aunt Henri needs those eggs."

We took off, pedaling down Cherry Lane. I expected Timbre Ann to pull ahead, but we rode side by side. We didn't talk any, but she kept looking over at me to be sure I was still there.

Seconds before we got to Sumter, the turnoff for the Piggly Wiggly, she veered left.

"Turn here. We're going to Fulbright's."

Fulbright's? Where in the blazes was that?

A steep hill loomed ahead of us. I grunted and leaned forward on my seat, trying to will my bike up the hill.

"The Pig's got to be closer," I said. The wind whipped my hair. A piece stuck to my sweaty cheek.

"C'mon," she said, "you can do it."

She kept along the route she was going, once standing up and letting the bike frame sway between her legs. I did the same. At the top of the hill, the road stretched out steady and straight. Tarnation. No downhill. No coasting. I had wanted to whiz by and make Timbre Ann laugh by sticking my hands behind my ears and crossing my eyes, calling, "Look, Timbre Ann, no hands."

Finally, she pulled off the side of the road and into a grove of trees. We bumped along on a dirt road until we came to a clearing.

"This is it?" I asked. Fulbright's was no bigger than a shed.

Timbre Ann leaned her bike against a peach tree.

"The eggs here are fresh. Mrs. Fulbright keeps chickens out back." She mopped her brow with one of Sam's kerchiefs. I stuck out my hand for her to pass it to me. "Yuck. Don't be gross, Polly."

Since when was sharing a sweat rag gross? We shared

Coca-Colas all the time. I turned my back to her, bent over, and used my shirt to wipe my face as she headed up the rickety front porch steps.

Fulbright's had no meat counter, but out back I spotted a few dead chickens hanging on a wire, ready to get plucked.

"Hey there, T.A.," the grocer-man said. He'd been stocking soup cans. *T.A.*? Timbre Ann never let me shorten her name. How come he got to? 'Cause he was colored?

"Hey, Peter," Timbre Ann said. "Hear you're going to be working at the shop. My pa said you're good. Born to be a mechanic."

"Mr. Biggs said that?"

This Peter character tossed the can of pea soup into the air and broke into a grin. Why, he was nowhere near a man's age. He was sixteen, seventeen at most. Then he saw me hanging back, farther down the aisle.

"Miss, can I help you with something?" he asked, all formal. "Directions to the main road?"

"Oh, she's with me." Timbre Ann didn't look like she knew what to do with her hands now that he noticed me. They fluttered about like those cartoon birds dancing around Snow White. "Peter, Polly. Polly, Peter."

Meemaw had taught me to shake hands, properlike, with the old biddies on the Ladies Auxiliary. I could see her lips sour-pucker at the very idea of me shaking this boy's hand.

"Nice to meet you, Peter," I said. My outstretched hand hung there. Dead weight, like those chickens out back. "I don't have cooties, you know."

Cooties. Peter bit his lip, trying not to laugh. Timbre Ann didn't hold back. She laughed loud and long. It was a stupid thing to say. A babyish thing to say. I knew it, but there was nothing I could do about it now.

I dropped my hand. "Forget it. Just trying to be nice was all."

Peter leaned in, gave me a handshake. "Sorry about that. Just can't be too careful. Not many white folks want to shake hands, least round here."

"Did your family get a flier, too?" Timbre Ann asked. She glanced around for a broken window, but she didn't spot one.

"Yeah."

"You closing?"

"No. No way." A cloud passed over Peter's face. "My father said it's bound to get worse before it gets better. Why it has to, I don't know."

"Me, neither," I said. Both Peter and Timbre Ann looked at me like I had no right to have any say-so. "What? Mama and I think of the Biggses as blood kin."

"Is that right?" Peter asked.

"Sure is," I said. I noticed Timbre Ann—T.A.—hadn't said what I hoped she would. *Tried and true. Polly's my best friend. Always was. Always will be.* Shoot, plenty of times I'd stuck up for her. Sally Jean and the others were always harassing me. Was she afraid Peter here would razz her for being friends with me?

"And what about your daddy?" Peter asked, his one brow raised.

"My daddy?"

"Yeah, you said your mama and you. You said nothing about your daddy."

I couldn't tell him Daddy was only a hair better than the rest. He tolerated the Biggses for Mama's sake.

Timbre Ann saved me. She piped up, "We better get going or Aunt Henri will have my hide." She liked Daddy about as much as Daddy liked her. She never said it, but I could see it in her shoulders the few times she'd been around him. "We need a dozen eggs, please."

"Sure. One sec."

Peter came back with them wrapped in a piece of heavy-duty fabric. No cardboard container like at the Piggly Wiggly.

"Won't they break that way?" I asked, as Timbre Ann stepped to the counter to pay. There was no cash register, but Peter unlocked a money box.

"No, they're fine," he said. "The bike basket should keep them safe. That is, if T.A. doesn't hit any potholes."

"I won't." She gave him the two quarters. His fingertips skimmed hers when he handed back the change.

"Peter, you gave me too much. Eggs are thirty cents or so."

He looked at the change she tried to hand back, a quarter, a dime and a nickel.

"Nope. For the pretty daughter of Mr. Sam Biggs, a dozen costs only ten cents, less than a penny an egg."

Lordy Lou, Timbre Ann blushed but good. Still, she held her hand out, that silver resting in her palm.

"Take it," she said. "I don't want it."

Peter looked hurtlike, as if he'd given Timbre Ann a dozen roses and she told him she didn't care for flowers.

"It's the Judge's money," Timbre Ann said, pocketing the correct change. "White folks don't deserve a discount."

ELEVEN
Bus Ride

I wanted to defend myself, to tell Timbre Ann that all white folks weren't the kind to throw bricks through windows, but she hadn't accused me of anything. Not out loud. So I let it be.

When we got back from Fulbright's, we settled in to do our homework. Henri started cracking and whipping egg whites for the soufflé while Mama took the pot roast and peas that she'd pureed special in the blender up to Miss Lily's room to feed her.

I was stuck on homework problem number two when the telephone rang.

"I'll get it," I said, hopping up.

"Anderson residence," I said into the phone, which was the way Mama told me the Judge liked his calls answered.

"Polly-gal, is that you?"

"Yessir," I said. *Daddy* I mouthed to Henri, since she

had stopped what she was doing to see who it was. Timbre Ann grunted and sharpened her pencil with one of those twisty sharpeners she kept in her patchwork pencil case.

"You and your mama take the bus tonight," he said. "I've got some business to take care of."

"Yessir." I couldn't question Daddy with Henri and Timbre Ann standing there. I hoped to high heaven that whatever "business" he was up to meant he was job hunting.

Mama was none too pleased to hear Daddy wasn't coming to carry us home. After Judge Anderson checked on his mother, we were free to go. Silently, we walked to the end of the block and waited for the bus to come. It arrived shortly after six P.M. It wasn't too crowded, so we took seats near the middle.

A few rows behind us, where the coloreds sat, there was a lady with her purse and hat on her lap. Beside her was a little boy. He swung his feet and sucked on a lollipop.

"Isn't he a happy boy," Mama said, setting the supper bag Henri sent us home with between her feet. She gave the boy a finger wave.

"Just got out of the dentist's office," the woman said. "No cavities. And what do they give him? Candy."

Mama laughed at that, her doesn't-that-beat-all laugh, and then she turned her attention to looking outside the window. Judge Anderson lived in a part-residential, part-business district that had doctors' offices and law offices housed inside some of the three-story and four-story homes. All had ornate gardens, with lilac bushes and fancy hedges.

It must've reminded Mama of all she had growing up. Pine Bluff was miles away, but Granddaddy worked two streets over from where Judge Anderson lived. His accounting firm was still standing.

There it was: Pritchard and McLean. The sign out front still bore his name.

Around the next corner, the bus hit a bump, a pothole or something, which was unusual in this part of town. The little boy behind us started wailing. He had louder lungs than both Aunt Clara's twins put together.

Up front, the passengers made faces, as if they smelled something foul.

"Shut him up," the bus driver shouted.

"Yessir," the woman said. She bounced the boy on her lap, but there was no consoling him. When we hit that pothole, he must've dropped his lollipop. He kept reaching for it, though his mother wouldn't let him have it. Bits of gravel and hair and Lord knows what else was probably stuck to it.

The colored women in the back searched through

their handbags, looking for something, anything, to keep the little boy quiet. All came up empty. No one had a sweet.

At the next stop, the driver got up and barreled his way down the aisle, past Mama, past me.

"Y'all are going to have to get off here," the driver said. He looked ashamed to be saying it, but he said it anyway.

"But we're nowhere near our stop," said the woman.

"Don't matter." The driver went to take her elbow, but she moved it, lightning quick.

"I don't . . ." Her voice cracked. She began again. "I don't . . . I don't have enough for another fare."

"Listen, gal, that ain't my problem. I just need you off this bus, and now." I could see the red creeping up his pale neck, like ketchup dribbled onto grits. "You're disturbing the other riders."

Why, this wasn't fair. Not fair at all.

The woman set her son, still bawling, down beside her. Hurriedly, she grabbed up her things. "Ssh, ssh, hush now," she told her son.

All the eyes that had been staring, making hateful glances, one by one, looked away. Big bullies. All of them. Just like Sally Jean. Just like whoever threw those bricks. I inched my butt off the seat and dug in my pocket for the nickel I knew was there. When we got back from Fulbright's, Henri gave it to me as payment for going with Timbre Ann to run to the store for the eggs the Judge needed.

"Polly." Mama put her hand on my arm. Her way of telling me no, to stay seated. I stayed where I was.

When the driver was satisfied the woman and her boy were leaving, he turned, made his way back to the front of the bus. I caught the lady just as she was about to get off.

"Here," I said. A nickel wouldn't stop Timbre Ann from seeing me as white girl first and as her forever-friend second, but I had to do something. "It's not a full fare but it's enough for a lollipop."

She took the nickel and stepped off the bus and onto the curb.

The bus driver grunted and the doors closed. I headed back to my seat, and now, all of those big bully eyes did their best to not look at me. Except for Mama's—hers lit into me like a match striking a flame.

"Don't you disobey me like that again," she said, tugging me by the ear back to my seat.

It wasn't like Mama to be rough like that. What had I done that was so bad? Her hand on my arm earlier was only for show. Not an order.

I picked at the dirt under my stubby fingernails. Just when I thought the tears would spill over and I'd be as snively as that little boy, the bus pulled to a stop. Our stop.

Our neighborhood had no curbs. The road wasn't paved. We stood in the scraggly grass and waited for the bus to chug along without us. I wanted to be anywhere, anywhere but beside Mama, even if it meant being back on that bus.

"Sorry to have sounded so sharp but things could have gone from bad to worse." Mama picked up my chin. "You did the right thing, baby-girl, but depending on who's watching—right can be wrong."

TWELVE
House Call

As we walked the three blocks home, I repeated Mama's words in my head: "depending on who's watching—right can be wrong." That was the stupidest thing I'd ever heard. Right was right, no matter what. Then I remembered what Timbre Ann once told me when we sat under our willow. About how she hated to see Sam hang his head and say "Yessir" to men she knew were nowhere near as good as him, but still he did it. He did it to keep her safe. I reckoned that's what Mama meant. I reckoned she meant to keep me safe.

Mama had moved on to other things. Namely, questioning me about Daddy.

"Your daddy didn't say where he was off to?"

"No, ma'am."

"Or why he'd be late?"

"No, ma'am."

"Or when he'd be home?"

"No, ma'am."

Lordy Lou, she'd already given me the third degree while Timbre Ann and I cleared our books off Judge Anderson's kitchen table.

As quick as she started in on me, Mama stopped. We hit Chessup Street. A patrol car was parked in our dirt driveway.

Sheriff Wilkes. What was he doing there?

"See the Judge has you working late," he said, as Mama and I got closer. He didn't get out of the car. He kept his arm on the rim of the open window. "His mama holding up?"

"About the same," Mama said, tight-lipped. She looked none too pleased to be making small talk with the Sheriff while our nearest neighbor, Mrs. O'Brien, shuffled her wash out to the laundry line. Chessup Street may not have any kids living on it other than me, but what it lacked in birthday parties and hopscotch squares, it made up for in busybodies and pinochle.

"Any idea where Otis is? Got some unfinished business with him."

Skinny Sheriff Wilkes looked nothing like the pot-bellied sheriffs shown on the nightly news, but he could still haul Daddy in.

"Well—um—," Mama stammered. She was never good at stalling. I was.

I jutted out my jaw. "He's out looking for a job."

"Is that right?" The Sheriff chuckled. He didn't bother getting out of his patrol car. "Good. Then he won't have trouble paying the fee Clara sent me to collect for a new paint job. Ask me, it was right nice to get me involved, versus dragging y'all into small claims court. But that's family for you—looking out for one another's best interests."

"How much?" Mama asked. She set the bag of left-overs on the ground and opened her handbag.

"Forty-three dollars." The Sheriff flicked his ciga-rette. The butt landed near my feet. "That's what the Buick dealer quoted. That's what you've got to pay."

Mama closed the clasp on her purse. "Don't carry that much on me. Polly, keep Sheriff Wilkes company. I'll just be a minute."

"Yes, ma'am," I said. As Mama hustled inside, she waved to Mrs. O'Brien like she had not a care in the world. I imagined Mama scurrying around behind the closed door, trying to round up a pile of bills. There was grocery money stashed in the coffee can above the sink, but I'd never seen more than ten or so dollars in there. Where would Mama round up that much cash?

"Seen you keeping company with that Biggs girl," Sheriff Wilkes said. "Ain't you too old to be playing with the likes of her?"

Another unwritten law: Give up all colored friends at the age of eight.

"Yessir," I mumbled, keeping my chin to my chest so "No damn business of yours" wouldn't tumble out.

"Good to hear." He patted me on the shoulder with his window-leaning arm. "Told your uncle you had plenty of Otis in you."

What did that mean? The Sheriff wasn't friends with Daddy. Not that I knew of. I kicked my feet, heel to toe, heel to toe. "I take after both Mama and Daddy."

"Well, you best find yourself a more suitable playmate."

I didn't take kindly to him ordering me around. I made sure Mama wasn't around to hear me. To tell me what I knew was right was wrong.

"Seventh grade is too old for playmates, Sheriff." This time I didn't mumble or hang my head.

The Sheriff raised his brow, sure he'd been sassed.

"Is that so? Well, sounds like it ain't just those inside the Tracks that need to be taught a lesson now, is it?"

Wasn't much I could say to that. I just stood there staring, knowing full well I'd crossed a line, and angered him but good.

When Mama returned, she draped her arm over my shoulder, protective-like, before handing the Sheriff a fat envelope.

"Here you are," she said. "Sorry you had to come all this way. I planned on stopping by Jimmy's store tomorrow."

"That so?" the Sheriff asked.

"My mama's not a liar."

Mama tightened her grip on my shoulder. "Polly, mind your tongue."

"Between Otis and this little spitfire here, Lisbeth, you sure got your hands full," the Sheriff said, laughing, though I suspect he didn't find me funny at all.

She gave me a little squeeze. "I certainly do," she said. "Polly gets lippy when she's hungry. I best get her fed."

"Not so fast." Why, Sheriff Wilkes had no intention of tucking that envelope in his glove compartment and wheeling off our property. He opened the envelope with his pointer finger and slid the wrinkled bills from one hand to the other. His lips moved as he counted.

"Ten, twenty," and then the ones, "twenty-one, twenty-two, twenty-three," until I could barely breathe. Finally he counted the very last bill: "forty-three."

"Anything else, Sheriff?" Mama asked. There wasn't one ounce of smug in her voice, but I saw it there in her eyes. Proud. Proud she'd had the money.

"No, ma'am. You enjoy your supper now." With the

roof of his patrol car inches above his head, Sheriff Wilkes did his best to tip his hat.

He got about halfway down our long dirt driveway before he stopped. "Polly," he called, motioning me over.

I didn't want to go, but Mama made me. "Mind that mouth," she said.

I neared the patrol car. "Yessir." I was close enough to smell the peanuts he'd been chomping.

"Good thing I have a funny bone," he said, tucking the money Mama gave him into his gun belt. "Trust me. You wouldn't want to make me mad."

"Yessir." I believed him. I'd pushed him far enough.

"Good, now go join your mama."

Backing away from his patrol car, I tripped over my own feet.

"And Lisbeth," the Sheriff said, raising his voice, though he didn't need to, "tell that husband of yours I got my eye on him, ya hear?"

Mama heard. I heard. Surefire, Mrs. O'Brien heard. She shook the same blasted sheet nearly a dozen times before pinning it to her line.

THIRTEEN

Baxter Bedtime

I sat glued to the television, glad it was Thursday and *Leave It to Beaver* was on. Despite the Beav's antics, I couldn't help but worry about the Sheriff's threat. Would something bad happen if I didn't stop being friends with Timbre Ann? And if so, what? To her or to me? Watching the clock made me all the madder. On the show, Mr. Cleaver, dapper in his cardigan, made it home each night for dinner, while mine couldn't tell suppertime from bedtime. Daddy was late. Way late.

I fell asleep with the television on.

"Hey there, Polly-gal, what are you doing up?" he asked, when he finally made it through the front door. He went to drop his keys in the chipped candy dish that I'd bought for a quarter at our church bazaar. He missed. They hit the floor.

"Ain't good for your eyes to sit in the dark like that." He turned on the lamp, but then squinted in the light. He turned it back off and plopped next to me on the sofa.

"Long day job hunting?" I asked.

"Could call it that. Teensy's itching to sell. He got a girl in Tallahassee . . ." Daddy's words trailed off. He cleared his throat. "In trouble. Yep, that's it. In trouble."

I yanked at a string on my cotton gown and crossed my arms over my belly. Wally and the Beav's dad would never use those words: "in trouble."

"Another week or so—if no one makes an offer," he grunted, struggling to pull off his boots. Had he been drinking? Meemaw could be like that, not so steady on her feet. She always blamed it on poor eyesight, but I bet she had 20/20 vision. Surefire, she watched me like a hawk.

"Let me." I crouched down to help him.

Daddy kept talking. "That's what I am hoping for. No offer. Then, why I bet Teensy will cut a chunk off his asking price. That's when I aim to make my move."

I wanted Daddy to be happy, but if I had a magic wand, I would've wanted more than that serving station. I'd put a spell on all us Baxters and turn us into a true-blue television family. Mama would serve meatloaf and wear pearls. Daddy would swing a briefcase and work downtown, and never, ever take a sip of whiskey. And no one, especially not the Sheriff, would care that Timbre Ann and I were friends.

"Imagine. Never having to work for a no-good boss

again," he said, wistful-like, before his voice turned sour. "Damn Foreman Taylor for firing me. If I've learned one thing, Polly-gal, it's that life ain't fair."

Was that why he started drinking? I was working the nerve up to ask when he changed the subject.

"Where's your mama? Reading?"

He struck a match. The fire flared as he lit his cigarette, a Lucky Strike.

"No, sir," I said, watching the smoke swirl above his head. "Mama wasn't feeling well. Took some milk of magnesia and turned in."

"Imagine your mama's face, her old man working for himself. Just like her father. Bet that would make Lisbeth proud. Don't you think?"

"Sure, Daddy."

I had thought things wouldn't be so topsy-turvy now that we were done with Meemaw and Sunday dinners, but they were worse. Mama sick in bed. Daddy'd gone out drinking. It all made me so mad, I gave Daddy's boot a tug with a twist. In nothing flat, I had it over his heel.

"What would I do without you, Polly-gal?" He ruffled my hair. Then he tucked his bootless foot under his behind and stretched the other—still booted—closer to me.

I wasn't about to yank the other one off. Not now. Now that I knew he'd come home drunk. I sat back on the sofa.

He left his other boot on.

"Any supper left?" he asked.

"Yessir."

He raised his brow at me. What? Was I supposed to be a waitress and heat it up for him, too?

"Henri packed us some pot roast and boiled peas," I managed to say.

Daddy stumped out his cigarette. "Your mama knows I don't like her taking food off the Judge's table. I can provide for my own."

"Mama grew up on Henri's cooking, is all," I said. I bit my pinky nail.

"Ain't Henri I got a problem with. She knows her place. It's that brother of hers," Daddy said. "Cutting into white folks' profits with that fool repair shop. Why, he's asking for trouble."

Daddy talking about Sam that way gave me a nail-on-the-chalkboard feeling. Sam had just as much right to make money as anyone else; that's what Mama said.

On television, they served coffee to sober folks up. I didn't know how to work the percolator, but maybe some food would help.

"Even cold, that pot roast was good. Sure you don't want some?" I asked.

"Is that meat what made your mama sick?"

"No, sir. Said her stomach felt fluttery. That she didn't feel like eating."

"That's not like your mama."

"Some stomach bug's been floating around school. Lots of kids are out sick."

"Hmm . . ." Daddy tugged off his other boot. He got up.

Maybe he wasn't as drunk as I first thought. He placed his boots near the front door. Old habits die hard. That's where he kept them when he worked at the mill.

"Mama said it was nothing retiring early wouldn't cure."

"That so?"

"Yep." I repeated our supper talk, verbatim—another of my vocabulary words, "word for word"—but plenty went unsaid. Stuff that Daddy would have needed to be there to decipher. How Mama had rubbed her stomach like she did mine when it wouldn't settle. And the strange look in her eyes when she said she'd better lie down. I reckoned that scene with the Sheriff sapped her energy, the same as it stole her appetite.

"You want to hear a secret?" Daddy plopped back beside me on the sofa. He tickled my ribs. The liquor had him loose. Playful. It was all I could do not to smile. I loved being tickled. "You do? Don't you?"

I laughed. I couldn't help it. Daddy hit all my tickle places. Underarms. Stomach. Sides. Elbows.

"Sure," I said, squirming.

"Well, me? I married your mama because I'd never seen such a pretty gal tear through three picnic plates of food and ask for more." He stopped the tickling but gave me a side hug. "Knew then she'd be my wife."

"When was that?" I asked. I'd been waiting for an in since that fight on the front porch. "High school? When you were a big-shot ball player?"

"Yep, way back then." He ran his palms over the scratchy stubble on his chin. He sounded sad, like his best years were behind him. He pulled himself off the sofa. Was he going to go to bed with Mama? Sleep beside her with his whiskey breath?

He stopped at the hall closet. Pulled out a bedsheet and returned, towering above me. The light of the television flickered like cracks of lightning in a storm, first bright, then dim.

"Best say g'night, Polly-gal. Lisbeth catches me stretching your bedtime, there'll be hell to pay," he said as he eased himself to reclining. I stood so he could spread out.

"Yessir."

"Good. Go wash up and then kiss me good night." He kicked the sheet over his stocking feet.

When I returned, he was snoring. Sound asleep or passed out, there'd be no waking him tonight.

On the way to my room, I cracked Mama's door. She slept on her back with her arms and legs taking up Daddy's side of the bed, like he'd never, not once, shared that space beside her.

FOURTEEN
Tender True

Mama wasn't better by morning. She looked gray. If I'd felt sick and that was my only symptom, Mama would have chided me with, "No fever, no missing school." For Mama to telephone Judge Anderson and explain that she'd be a no-show, and that Henri would have to take care of Old Lady Lily, meant Mama wasn't fibbing. To skip a day's pay, she was sick, wore out, or both.

The school day passed lightning quick. With half the class out sick, including smart-mouthed Sally Jean, Miss Kilburn gave us silent reading time. Lost in *The Adventures of Tom Sawyer*, I flipped pages trying to keep up with Tom and Becky as they ran from Injun Joe.

When the dismissal bell rang at 3:10 PM, I shoved the book in my desk and hightailed it to the willow. I stashed a note for Timbre Ann in the gnarled knot, telling her to go on to the Andersons without me. After the Sheriff's warning, it wouldn't do for either of us to lollygag at our special spot.

I tore home to check on Mama, running the whole way. Out of breath, I doubled over when I reached our drive, Daddy's truck was parked where it was when I left that morning.

Why wasn't he out job hunting? Was he hung over? Still drunk?

I slipped into the house. The living room was empty. Kitchen, too. I grabbed a handful of Saltines from the open package on the counter and went to check on Mama. Her door was cracked to let in the afternoon air. I peeked inside. What I saw made my heart hurt.

Mama and Daddy lay in their bed, her head cradled against his chest. He stroked her hair and sang her that "Love Me Tender" song she loved.

I closed the door, feeling silly for doubting Daddy at all.

FIFTEEN
Hear, Hear

It took a whole week—seven days—of listening to Daddy's love songs, sipping chicken broth, and sucking ice cubes before Mama beat that stomach bug. I got so used to seeing Daddy at the stove, it surprised me when Mama was up and dressed Friday morning, frying eggs and the last of the potatoes we had in the pantry. Not once during all that time had I seen him take a drink, but he must've been sipping on the sly. More than once, while Mama napped for long stretches, his breath had smelled sticky sweet, but foul all the same. I never told Mama. I hoped she'd be none the wiser.

"Hope you're hungry, sugar." Mama sipped her coffee with one hand and scooped me in for a hug with the other, kissing the top of my head. Meanwhile, Daddy read the newspaper. "Big day today, with me going to ask Judge Anderson for a raise. Think he'll say yes?"

"Um . . . ," I stalled. Mama's timing, asking for more

money after she hadn't shown up for a week, seemed off to me. But with Mama all hopeful, waiting on an answer, I didn't want to be the one to drain the color from her cheeks.

"Sure, Mama," I said. "Sure."

I settled into my chair, reassuring myself I hadn't set Mama up to get shot down. Judge Anderson wasn't Meemaw mean. He could be kindly when he wanted to, like letting Henri and Mama carry home leftovers. I reckoned he was just as likely to say yes as he was to say no. Fifty-fifty odds weren't half bad.

" 'Course you'll get it. You deserve it," Daddy said, folding the newspaper lengthwise.

Done with that morning's *Holcolm Sentinel*. He spread it on the floor, near his feet. The headline read WAREHOUSE FIRE. And there was a photo of a Negro man shaking his head. Had he gotten one of those same letters wrapped around a brick that the Biggses and the Fulbrights had gotten? I wanted to steal the newspaper up off the floor, but Daddy had started using a butter knife to chip the mud off his boots, with the paper underneath to keep the Georgia clay from dirtying the floor.

"If the Judge says no, tell him you'll refuse to clip Old Lady Lily's toenails so *he* has to do it. That should seal the deal."

I'd have to find out more about the fire later. There was no way I could do it now.

"Got an interview today?" I asked. Last time Daddy cleaned his mud-caked boots was when he got hired on at the mill to cut and load lumber.

"Could call it that. Got a meeting. A business meeting."

"With who?" Mama asked, serving up our plates.

"That's for me to know and you to find out." Daddy winked. "Teensy's?" I mouthed when Mama couldn't see. Daddy nodded.

"Fine," said Mama. "You and Polly keep your secret." She looked like Eddie Haskell from *Leave It to Beaver* when he gave Wally the business. "Maybe I've got one of my own. Now we best say grace before breakfast gets cold. Polly?"

I bowed my head. "Rub a dub dub, thanks for the grub. Yay God."

"Amen," Daddy said. He hit his thigh with his palm. "To a raise for your mama."

"And to your daddy's *business* meeting." Mama arched her brow, a reminder she'd only let Daddy keep his secret for so long before she started asking questions. She lifted her cup to meet his.

"I'll drink to that," I said. Maybe a toast had the power to make wishes come true, like spotting a shooting star. I raised my milk cup higher. "To better days for us Baxters."

"Hear, hear," Mama and Daddy echoed, their voices mixing with mine.

SIXTEEN
Front-Page News

For the first time that week, I met Timbre Ann at our willow. I had my latest list of vocabulary words already out of my notebook, ready for her to quiz me. When I saw her coming, though, I knew there'd be no quiz time today, nor any racing. She stared at her feet, not even waving when she saw me. When I asked her what was wrong, she showed me the front-page story I only got a glimpse of that morning.

"Electrical fire, my foot," said Timbre Ann. "Mr. Castle wanted to buy that gas station that sits at the edge of the Tracks."

"Teensy's?" I asked. Heavens, there was no way the Klan or the Council would let that happen. Daddy, neither. *He* wanted to buy Teensy's.

"They're trying to shut us down. Close us down," Timbre Ann said, as I scanned the article.

The Negro man, whose crumpled face I remembered

peeking out from under Daddy's boot flakes, looked tore up. The paper said half his door-to-door vacuum cleaner inventory had been lost in the warehouse fire. It also reported some colored businesses were thriving and it named half a dozen—some in direct competition with white-owned businesses. Biggs Repair was one of them.

"Why? Because your places are making money?" I asked.

"Cash is cash, even to the Citizens Council," Timbre Ann said. "Pa thinks they meant it as an example. To let colored businesses know they don't like Negroes cutting into their profits."

The night that Daddy had come home late, he'd said much the same thing about Sam.

"Are folks at your church looking into it?" I asked Timbre Ann. The Sheriff wasn't, I'd bet.

"Yeah, but it could have been anyone," Timbre Ann stared at the article. What she really wanted to say, but didn't, was "anyone white." "Some folks think the Sheriff was in on it, but Pa said not to jump to any conclusions."

With the mention of the Sheriff, I ushered Timbre Ann along our usual path. What was it he'd said? *"It ain't just those inside the Tracks that need to be taught a lesson, is it, Polly?"* Yep, that was it. Was he just trying to scare me, or was he for real?

My gut flip-flopped as Timbre Ann and I walked through the woods, past the ravine, to Judge Anderson's yard. Along the way, I learned plenty.

While Mama had been out sick, Dennis Castle drove in from two towns over to sell his wares to the folks who lived inside the Tracks. Timbre Ann played with Rufus, his mangy mutt, while Henri paid cash money for a Fairfax S-1, which was tons bigger than Aunt Clara's Flying Gernsbackian vacuum that looked like an alien from outer space. Lots of other folks bought stuff, too.

It seems the Sheriff, who never patrolled the Tracks, decided to keep an eye on things that day, of all days. Or Teensy may have phoned the Sheriff to tell him about that Castle fella. Either way, Mr. Castle was pulled over. He got a ticket, for a broken taillight. Which hadn't been broken before the Sheriff pulled him over, from the way those at Mount Zion, Timbre Ann's church, had been telling it.

"He told him not to step foot back in Holcolm," Timbre Ann said. "But Mr. Castle did. He came back the next day to deliver some vacuums. Then, that night, there was the fire."

We neared the end of the woods. We were still a ways away, but I could spot Mama and Henri milling about in the Andersons' kitchen. Good—they were safe. No one would touch Mama or Henri at the Judge's house.

"What about Biggs Repair?" I asked. "Is Sam in danger?"

"Maybe. Most likely." Timbre Ann sighed. She must've had a lot more on her mind than schoolwork. "Pa said, 'I'm not closing my doors. Not even if pigs fly. Not even if the town pillars stage a sit-in.' "

"The pillars?"

Timbre Ann looked at me like I'd gotten a big fat zero on my spelling test. "You know, white folks like your aunt and uncle. Like Mrs. Pritchard. *Respectable* members of Holcolm society."

"Ha, I'd pay to see that," I said.

Sam was right. That would never happen. The very idea of Meemaw dirtying her big behind in her Ladies Auxiliary suit at a protest, surefire, that was a hoot. But whoever set that fire didn't mean to have folks laughing. He meant to have them running scared.

SEVENTEEN
According to Plan

That afternoon, Mama and Henri chatted while Timbre Ann and I sat at the Andersons' kitchen table finishing our snack, an apple. Today was Mama's first day back to work. Miss Lily had pitched a fit in Mama's absence. She didn't mind eating the food Henri cooked and then pureed special in a blender, but she didn't want any coal-black hands wiping her lily-white bottom. Even after news of the fire, Henri acted like Old Lady Lily had every right to be a bigot.

"I know my worth," she said. "When my day comes, the Lord above is going to welcome me with open arms."

"Well, I know where Miss Lily's going," I said, wrapping my arms around Henri's middle. "And it isn't up to heaven with you."

"Hush, Polly. You want her to hear you?" Mama said. She came around Henri and swatted me on the behind with her hand towel. She'd been helping Henri polish the silver

103

while Old Lady Lily napped. "You two best get started on your homework."

While Timbre Ann and I spread out our schoolbooks, Henri got out the flour. Tonight she was making dumplings. The chicken was already boiling in a pot on the stove. Mama tossed a load of laundry in the Judge's washer, bought—where else—at Uncle Jimmy's store.

I got out my math book. Miss Kilburn had postponed our review test since that flu had been hopping around, keeping kids out for the better part of two weeks. The delay gave me time to practice. I didn't want to, but I was determined to get good at long division. Algebra was up next, and, surefire, I didn't want to fall behind.

After math, I tackled spelling and then history. Timbre Ann was still at it, her head bent over her geography book, twisting one of her braids, so when I finished my paragraph on the importance of the cotton gin, I got busy helping Mama.

"Least Miss Lily is scrawny," I said, holding up one of the fresh-from-the-dryer cloth diapers. "Meemaw would need three of these thingies stitched together to cover her big behind."

Mama snatched the diaper right out of my hands. "Your grandmother is fully capable of going to the bathroom by herself."

Shoot—I knew that. No need for her to get so huffy.

"And it isn't a joke that Miss Lily can't," Mama added.

"You can say that again," Henri chimed in from where she stood, her hip solid against the floured counter. "Ain't nothing funny about bodily functions—young or old. You get to be Timbre Ann's age, you'll realize that, sure enough."

Henri paused. Got that "mercy do I have something to tell you" look.

"Goodness me, Lisbeth, how could I have forgotten . . ." Henri trailed off, full of excitement. "My niece here, why, she's all grown!"

Mama clapped her hands. She jumped out of her chair, ran around the table, and hugged Timbre Ann.

"Congratulations," Mama said. She patted Timbre Ann on the back like she'd earned herself a blue ribbon. For what? Being grown? She didn't look taller to me.

"How're you? Are you in any pain?" Mama rattled off question after question. "Don't worry, before long, you'll get used to it. The price we women pay," Mama said, like Timbre Ann had joined their club. Hers and Henri's.

Lordy Lou, she had.

Timbre Ann had gotten her period. Her first period.

She shifted in her seat something fierce, as Mama and Aunt Henri talked about how old they were when "Aunt Flo" came to call. For Timbre Ann, it came late. Mama and Henri got theirs at thirteen. They reminisced, going back in time like it was yesterday. I reckoned Timbre Ann'd had enough of the girly talk. Without warning, she shut her geography book. "All done. C'mon, Polly, let's go outside."

"Tidy up. Judge Anderson likes things neat as a straight pin," Mama reminded me when I got up from the table without stacking my schoolbooks.

Tarnation. Between the fire and the hoopla over Timbre Ann's period, I'd forgotten all about Mama asking Judge Anderson for a raise. Mama hadn't. She threaded her fingers together, a sure sign she was nervous as all get out.

"Yes, ma'am," I said, and mouthed "good luck" as I slid my chair neatly under the table before scooting outside.

I reckoned I couldn't fault Timbre Ann for keeping secrets; these days I had plenty of my own. I decided not to bring it up as we made our way outside. Now that it was October, that late-September heat spell had broken. The sun was shining. It was warm, but not humid—perfect weather for my favorite game.

"Hide-and-seek," I announced, like Timbre Ann had been sitting on her hands, waiting for me to come up with a plan. "I'll count to one hundred while you hide. And no going inside. Mama and Henri want us out of their hair."

"What about hula hooping?" Timbre Ann asked. She'd already headed to the shed. The Judge let me stash a few things in there: a hula hoop, a jump rope, and some jacks. "Hide-and-seek is babyish."

"Is not."

"Is so."

"Is not." Sheesh, I sounded seven going on six. I tried another tactic. "Studies are your strong suit. Fun is mine. Now, are we going to waste time arguing, or what?" Before Timbre Ann could answer, I leaned against the house, covered my eyes with my arm, and began counting. "One Mississippi, two Mississippi, three—"

Timbre Ann sighed. "Have it your way." Then she darted off to my left.

When I got to eighty-eight Mississippi, I heard Judge Anderson whistle, his evening ritual at the end of his walk home from the courthouse. I kept counting, afraid that Timbre Ann would come out of hiding if she heard my voice trail off. I scooted under the parlor window, away from the kitchen where Henri ran the faucet, washing the dirty dishes from her afternoon's work. Mama's timing and mine couldn't have been better.

"Ready or not, here I come," I called. I pushed away from the house and then ran back to the window to listen in on the conversation between Mama and the Judge. I'd find Timbre Ann as soon as Mama got the A-okay.

"Judge, you are a fair man, more than fair and I, umm . . . I want you to know I enjoy, a-huh, umm . . . more than enjoy working for you and umm . . . caring for your mother."

I grimaced. Mama did a whole lot more *umming* and *ahuhing*. Finally, she got it out. Seven dollars. A whole seven dollars more every other week. I bit my lip, imagining Mama in the parlor doing the same, while we both waited for Judge Anderson's answer.

"Lisbeth, I appreciate all you do for Mother. I'll gladly give you a raise."

My chest pumped as big as a balloon. How it did that on the exhale, I didn't know, but it did.

"But . . ."

"But"? He'd said yes. Why was he still talking?

". . . to do so I'll have to cut Henri's pay. Not a whole fourteen dollars, mind you, but at least seven or eight." Judge Anderson cleared his throat. Though I couldn't see him, I'd bet he was running his starched white hanky across his forehead, patting it dry. "Now, Lisbeth, when you tell her, just inform her that as a household, we have to cut back, and that includes a slight change in her compensation."

I pounded my fist into the brick—not hard, but enough to scrape my skin.

"From what I hear, income from her brother's shop can make up the difference," the Judge said. "It's a crying shame when hardworking whites aren't as well off as their Negro counterparts. Isn't it?"

The Judge had just about spelled it out, just like that hateful flier. Sam's shop was doing well, so Henri needed taking down a peg.

Mama did her best to recover. "Why, why, I, umm . . . ," she mumbled, "I could get by with three or four dollars more a week. Saving for a new vacuum. That's plenty raise enough."

"Now, Lisbeth, you don't need a new vacuum, do you?"

How did the Judge know we didn't have wall-to-wall carpeting, but throw rugs I beat over the banister with a switch? Or was he making a sly remark about Henri buying one from that salesman? Did everyone know the goings-on inside the Tracks?

"No, sir." She sounded as if all hope had been wrung out of her.

"Well, in that case, you won't be needing a raise at

all, will you?" With those words, the Judge might as well have pounded his gavel. Court dismissed.

"Ready or not, here I come," I called.

Timbre Ann wasn't under the back porch. She wasn't crouching behind a lawn chair. Nope. When I found her, she was behind the shed, hula hooping, not hiding, like she'd wanted to do all along.

EIGHTEEN
Playing It Safe

Better days weren't ahead for us Baxters, better nights neither. That evening, when Sam came to pick up Henri and Timbre Ann, Mama decided it was best I go with them so she could break the no-raise news to Daddy on her own.

"Be good," Mama said, as she clutched her pocketbook to her side. "And don't worry. Your daddy will understand."

"Sure, Mama." How could he understand? Surefire, Mama wouldn't tell him the gospel truth. That she wouldn't take money from the Biggses' pocket to put into ours. Would she?

When we climbed in the car, Sam, despite the news from the newspaper, was his usual friendly self.

"Is it WKTO you like?" Sam asked, hand at the ready to twist the dial to 102.3.

"Yessir," I said. Even though I didn't have to call Sam "sir," I did. "But leave what you've got on. I haven't heard this song before."

"Oh, I love this song." Timbre Ann tapped her foot.

I didn't know the name of it, but the beat sure was catchy. Sam started singing along and Henri joined in, clapping like we were in church. Timbre Ann elbowed me. She let out a family-is-family laugh before joining in. I listened to their voices blend together. Sam's dark as molasses, Henri's almost as deep, and Timbre Ann's higher, and slightly off pitch, like a teakettle letting out a whistle.

My whole soul wanted to sing along. The chorus was easy enough. But I couldn't work up the nerve. I'd sound like Polly Is a Cracker Baxter.

When the song ended, a commercial for Uncle Jimmy's store, Whitmire Appliance, came on: "where brand-new Frigidaires, televisions, and toasters are all on sale." Sam turned down the volume before Aunt Clara gave directions, like folks in Holcolm County didn't know where Main Street was.

"Hey, Polly," Timbre Ann said, shifting her schoolbooks, "after supper, do you want to see my coin collection?"

"Sure."

"I've still got that 1928 quarter you found not far from the willow. It's sparkly now that I've cleaned the mud and guck off," Timbre Ann said. "Oh, and wait till you see. Pa built me a display case like the one at Woolworth's. But better. With fancy glass doors and everything."

"Really? Truly?" I asked, sounding like snotty Sally Jean, fingering Beverly's new hair ribbons. "I'd give anything to have a display case. I worry about my nests falling apart."

"Nests?" Sam asked, his eyes narrowing. I caught sight of them in the rearview mirror.

"Yep," I said. "I collect them."

Sam nodded at me to go on. I might as well tell him. I loved my nests something fierce.

"Some have sticks poking out, or the mud patty is so dry it's cracked. They're the neatest things, each so different. It's all I can do to stop myself from climbing up a tree and staying there to see exactly how they're made."

"Why, Polly," Henri said, "you sound like Sam did when he was your age, noticing stuff with an artist's eye."

"I'm no artist," Sam said. "I'm a businessman."

"You're both, Pa," Timbre Ann said. "Your woodwork and your whittling should go in some kind of museum. They're that good."

From the side I saw Sam smile. He looked happy as all get out that Timbre Ann was proud of his handiwork.

"Not just anyone can handle nests," I said. "You've got to be gentle with them or they fall apart. I keep mine in a lined dresser drawer."

"Sounds like you need a display case," Sam said.

I half hoped he'd offer to build me one, and maybe he would've if Henri hadn't cut in.

"Brother, watch that speedometer," Henri said. "We got company."

A patrol car that had been hiding behind patches of dense bushes pulled out behind us. Sheriff Wilkes.

The two-lane stretch of highway was deserted. The Sheriff pulled out behind Sam and quickly pulled over to pass, ignoring the fact that there was no dotted white line saying he could, but a double line saying he could not. Without being told, I slid as far under the backseat as I could. If the sheriff was going to give Sam a ticket, he would've flipped on his lights. Why, he had to be barreling along beside us to run us off the road.

"Stay calm," Sam instructed. "There's a turnoff coming."

Sam edged on the brake, popped his turn signal on, and slowly, casually, turned onto Rural Route 5, just as the Sheriff was closing in, I suspected.

I closed my eyes, bracing for the worst, when a loud horn—not sirens—blared.

"What happened?" My voice shook.

"That semi coming over the hill brought the Sheriff's attention back where it belonged," Sam said. "On the road."

I slid back onto the seat, using my elbows for leverage. "Good driving, Sam."

"Stay down," Henri snapped at me. "We ain't out of the clear yet. He could double on back."

I made myself as small as I could. "Sorry y'all got saddled with me."

"Hush, this has nothing to do with you," Sam said.

But it did. Carrying a white girl, one the Sheriff had already threatened for befriending Negroes, would just add fuel to the Sheriff's fire. I truly hoped he hadn't seen me.

NINETEEN
Look-Alike

The part of the Tracks where the Biggses lived was nowhere near as run-down and forlorn looking as Chessup Street. I didn't spot any sagging porches or shutters with peeling paint. The house at the end of Timbre Ann's block was as unsightly as it ever got, but all it needed was a good weeding around the mailbox and to have its grass cut. It could be spiffed up in a jiff.

We pulled into Timbre Ann's drive. If I hadn't been halfway raised at Pine Bluff, I would've thought the Biggses' place could pass for a hoity-toity home. Window boxes hung from every window. The wraparound porch, painted a pine-tree green, looked as pretty as any picture in *The American Home Magazine*.

There was no need to park the car on the front lawn; they had an aluminum carport to boot. Sam pulled the car under it. First-class service, for sure.

"Get on inside now," said Henri. She used her big

body to block me, figuring the Sheriff might still be on our tail.

I'd only been to the Biggses' a handful of times, the last time being four years ago when Timbre Ann and I both had chicken pox. We weren't sure who got them first, me or her. Not that it mattered. Daddy was a truck driver then, away on an overnighter, and Mama had a test in her nursing class that she couldn't miss, so she made arrangements for me to spend the night.

Surefire, I was all red faced and itchy, but even more I remembered building a fort out of couch cushions with Sam while Timbre Ann got her bath.

"Fancy that," he'd said, when the last sheet was draped over the back of Henri's chair. "You're a real builder."

"Think so?" I asked.

"Know so." He scooped me up and tossed me inside. He smelled like the underside of a car hood and Ivory soap. Different than Daddy. Daddy smelled of endless cups of coffee and fried food. If he wore cologne it could have been named "Ode to the Road."

"What are y'all doing?" Timbre Ann asked when she came back from her bath.

"Polly built you two a healing tent." Sam kissed Timbre Ann good night. I waited for my good-night kiss, but it never came. I realized later that Sam couldn't have kissed me. Not me—a white girl. "Now, no scratching can go on in here. You got that?"

"Yes, Pa."

"Yessir."

Sam darkened the room, turning off the lamps one by one, before going to have his after-supper coffee with Henri. Their voices carried from the kitchen; though they sounded close by, they eventually faded altogether. As soon as we heard the silence, Timbre Ann sat up.

We scratched each other like alley cats with a bad case of fleas. When we were all scratched out, we flopped back on the blankets. In my ear, Timbre Ann asked, "Polly, be my sister?"

"I'll be your sister," I whispered back.

"Good, then you can sleep over every night."

She curled her legs around mine and I couldn't have left, even if I'd wanted to.

Now, nothing about the Biggses' house looked the way it had then: well-kept but worn, like our pillbox house. Since I'd last been back, they had redecorated. Red hens darted the walls, the kind of wallpaper I expected to see in a restaurant. The counters looked spit shined, or buffed with some of that wax Sam used on the cars he serviced at Biggs Repair. And on the wall was a tick-tocking clock made from an honest-to-goodness tree stump. Sam's latest handiwork, I imagined.

Henri set the leftover chicken and dumplings she'd made at the Andersons on the stove to warm.

"Supper won't be long. You two, go wash."

I was as used to following Henri's orders as I was to scuttling behind Timbre Ann. We rounded a corner and went down a long hallway to Timbre Ann's very own bathroom, one she didn't have to share with anyone but me.

Timbre Ann washed up, then handed me the soap. It was bubbly from her scrubbing. I washed good, singing my ABCs in my head, which Mama told me was the right amount of time to scrub up. Timbre Ann waited, ready to hand me a towel.

"What?" I asked. She stared at me. Was I washing funny?

"Nothing," Timbre Ann said.

"No, that look was something," I said. Was she worried about Sheriff Wilkes? I hadn't told her about his coming to the house, issuing me a warning. I told myself that because of dealing with Mama and Daddy, I'd never gotten around to it. But the truth was, I didn't want to have her think any worse of white folks than she already did. Whatever was going on, surefire, someone as pale as me was in on it.

"Just never noticed how much you look like Mrs. Pritchard, is all."

I snatched that towel from her. "Do not."

The last thing I wanted was to resemble Meemaw in any way. Being blood related to her was bad enough.

"Yeah, around the eyes," Timbre Ann said. She didn't say it meanlike, but surprised. "But your mama has them, too. They're pretty."

"Really?"

I knew for sure I had Mama's coloring, pale with freckles, but I never gave a thought to whose eyes I had.

I looked in the mirror. Surefire, there were both Meemaw's and Mama's green-flecked hazel eyes.

"Wonder what I got from Daddy?" I asked, seeing no traces of him looking back at me.

Timbre Ann went to flick off the bathroom light. "Let's hope not a thing."

I grabbed her arm. "What's that supposed to mean?"

"Nothing." She glanced at my hand, pale against her skin.

I let her go. I hadn't meant to grab her. "Don't you lie to me. You meant something."

Timbre Ann turned to the doorway like she half hoped Henri or Sam would be standing there to get her out of what she'd started.

"You know, his temper," Timbre Ann said. "Getting fired for hitting that fella so hard he almost lost his eye."

That's what got Daddy fired? Not a word fight but a fistfight? I stood a little straighter. Acted like I knew that fight was bad—as bad as it was. So long as she didn't know about the drinking.

TWENTY
Pit Stop

Sam must've carried me, sound asleep, to the car. At about nine-thirty, when Mama still hadn't come to get me, I closed my eyes. I hadn't meant to doze. No way, no how, did I want to spend the night at Timbre Ann's. Not after what she'd said about Daddy.

I woke slumped in the front seat of Sam's sedan. I stayed quiet. He was taking me home. Out the windshield, I could see the tops of the trees, the pine branches reaching to the midnight sky. Watching them, I drifted back off.

When we stopped, we were parked in front of Biggs Repair.

"Sam," I said, yawning, "aren't you taking me home?"

"Shhh, go back to sleep," Sam said. "We'll be at your house soon. This is just a pit stop. I need to run inside and get something."

Soft as he could, Sam closed the door and slid out into

the night. He left the engine running and the headlights on, proof that what he said was true. He wouldn't be long. Alone, I got a case of the heebie-jeebies. It felt like something was out there, out in the trees watching. Was it the Sheriff? Or my imagination?

I sleep-stumbled to the same door Sam had gone through. Once in the garage, I almost bumped into a '57 Ford Fairlane up on cinder blocks. Daddy loved the Fairlane. He always dreamed of having one. I ran my hand along the tailfins as I moved toward the back of the store. Biggs Repair was built inside an old barn, and the front was where Sam worked on cars. The back was where he took apart air conditioners, alarm clocks, toasters and such, and got them all working again.

It was dark. Sam hadn't turned any lights on, save the one coming from the office. I followed the dim light until I stood in the doorway, happy I had made it without crashing into anything.

I didn't see him anywhere. No—there he was, hunched over, crouched below his desk.

"Sam," I said softly, hoping he wouldn't chastise me. He'd told me to wait in the car, but it was spooky out there. It was spooky in here, too.

"Gracious sakes. You scared the devil out of me." He stood and strained, lifting an iron safe about the size of a bread box, but much heavier, and set it on the desk. "I'll just be a minute. Neither us, nor this money, is safe here at this time of night."

I came closer.

"I could kick myself for not taking it earlier," he said. He moved money from one hand to the other lightning quick. I couldn't rightly tally how much, but it was plenty more than we kept in our coffee can. "I thought it'd be safer here than at home, but I've had this nagging in my gut all night."

"What about a bank?" I asked. We didn't have piles of money like Meemaw or Sam, but Mama made a deposit and a withdrawal each payday.

"Most of my kin stash their money around the house, in old books, under mattresses, but I always thought that was superstitious. Money needs to be locked up. But not here, not anymore. The Sheriff followed me for a reason, and I am not closing shop, but I'll be damned if I don't protect my family."

He tapped a stack of cash on the desk, grabbed an envelope, and stuffed the money inside. It wouldn't all fit. A felt pouch lay near the Bible. He dumped his whittling tools and stuffed the envelope and the rest of the money inside. His hands shook.

In the car and over dinner, Sam acted like all would

be fine, that the brick and the Sheriff following us was no big deal. But it *was* a big deal. Sam was scared.

He tucked the pouch into his waistband. Not on his hip, where the Sheriff hung his holster, but around back. "Got to pray for the best and expect the worst. In the meantime, I've got to find a safer spot for my girl's college fund."

I should have known all that money was for Timbre Ann. It wasn't twigs, but it was a nest all the same.

He stood, clicked on a flashlight, and then turned off the desk lamp. "C'mon now, we best get you home."

Sam held out his hand and I took it. He led me out of the store. On the way, we passed the broken window where that brick must've come flying through. A piece of plywood was nailed over it. Seeing it, I shivered.

TWENTY-ONE
Going, Going, Gone

On the weekends, Daddy liked to play short-order cook. His home fries tasted better than Daisy's down at the diner, but his specialty was flapjacks. He flipped them without a spatula, nothing but a pan and a flick of his wrist. But this morning, Daddy wasn't at the stove. He was nowhere near the kitchen.

Mama yanked the refrigerator so hard that the handle almost came off. She scanned the contents. "Dammit. We're out of milk."

She closed the refrigerator and opened the cupboard. "Dry rice cereal fine with you?" she asked.

I hated rice cereal. With milk they were bad enough, but dry they resembled the lice found in Jacob Jackson's hair every school year. "Can't we have eggs?"

"None left. It's dry cereal or toast."

"Toast," I said, opening the store brand I hated. I preferred Wonder Bread. Soft, mushy, and white. "At least that's hot."

Mama poured a cup of coffee and took her seat at the table. She tapped her sugar spoon like a war drum.

"I'll make you some, too," I offered. That should calm her. I reckoned she had a right to be riled. When Sam dropped me off, long after midnight, Daddy still wasn't home. Mama said he'd been plenty peeved about her not getting that raise, but not enough to miss his weekly poker game, which had grown in importance since Daddy still didn't have a job.

Maybe by the time Mama had a bite or two of toast, Daddy would wake up. He'd toss his keys in the air and make a run to town for eggs, milk, bacon, and Bisquick. After one of his "Saturday-morning specials," he'd kiss Mama on the nape of her neck, and-raise or not, staying out late or not—we Baxters would be back to normal.

While I slid the bread into the toaster, Mama pulled out her makeup bag from her pocketbook. Reckon if Daddy didn't wake soon, Mama planned to take the truck and go get the groceries herself.

"Can I come shopping?" I asked, as I cut the toast on a diagonal, the same way Mama served it, and laid our plates on the table. "I need paste and cotton balls for school. Miss Kilburn is teaching a lesson on the boll weevil and we've got to make a display."

I didn't mention that Miss Kilburn let the class pick

pairs, and—surprise, surprise—no one picked me. Sally Jean and Beverly giggled at my predicament, but for once Miss Kilburn came to my rescue. She announced, "Polly's vocabulary scores, four one hundreds in a row, have proven to me that she is capable enough to work on her own. Good work, Polly." It'd almost be worth it to tell Mama about my slight just to parrot the words, "Good work, Polly," but before I could decide whether my story would put Mama in a better mood, she cut off my train of thought.

"I'm not running to the store today."

"I thought you said—"

"I said we need groceries but your daddy's God knows where with the truck." Mama's voice rose like bath water. "Even if we took the bus, what are we going to pay with—our good looks?"

"Isn't there enough—" I stopped midsentence, my eyes trailing over to the coffee can in the cupboard.

"It's empty. What little there was in the coffee can is gone, and your daddy along with it." She went from angry to stone cold. "He didn't come home last night, Polly."

My throat burned. Didn't come home?

"He could be hurt," I said. Hadn't she thought of that? "He could've had an accident." Tarnation, Mama. If he'd been out drinking he could be—dead.

"Serves him right if he did get in a wreck," Mama muttered more to herself than to me.

I hopped up and went to the counter. I searched for the Yellow Pages in one drawer after another. I smacked the book on the counter. "I'm calling the hospital."

"You will not, young lady. I'll handle this." She wrenched the phone book from me.

I wrestled her for it, but I let go almost as quick. She rocked back on her heels, hitting her back on the edge of the counter. I crossed my arms over my chest, trying to lock myself up tight.

"This wouldn't have happened if you would've taken that raise," I said. "Done what Judge Anderson asked."

"How did you know about that?" Mama rubbed her back where the counter gouged her. I hadn't meant to hurt her. Honest. "Polly Beatrice Baxter, I did not raise you to spy on folks."

"The Biggses don't need the money," I said, stopping shy of telling her about the pit stop Sam made on the way home. "We do. How come you didn't think of that?"

That slowed Mama. She slid the wrinkled phone book back in the drawer.

"You've got a right to be upset, little miss, but I will not have you back talking me. Understand?"

I sank to my seat. The nibbles I'd made in my toast re-sembled a mouse's—small and scared.

"Yes, ma'am."

"Despite having no food in this house, I am still your mother." She glanced out the window above the sink. Back to where the fields gave way to the Tracks. "As for this morning, I called Henri and she insisted, she is sending Sam over with the car. He's going to carry me to Pine Bluff."

What? Hadn't they told her about the Sheriff? About his trailing us? Mama was asking for it. Things were getting scary.

"No!" I jumped up so hard my heels hurt.

"That's enough, Polly," Mama said, pointing at my chair. "If a bus ran all the way out there, I'd take it. Henri and Sam are doing us a favor. We should be grateful."

I stayed standing. It wasn't Sam and Henri I was mad at. It was Mama for always leaning on them. "But we're better off without Meemaw."

"Polly, I am not going to argue with you about this." Mama pointed again at my chair.

I sat down. "But—"

"I talked it over with Henri. That night at Sunday dinner, our actions, all our actions, were downright shameful," Mama said. "It's time I issue Mother an apology. Only then will she give me enough to get us through."

"Don't, Mama," I pleaded, lacing my legs around the

chair so I wouldn't hop out. "Daddy won't be the least bit happy when he finds out."

"Your father's not blind; he has to know your grand-mother has been spotting us cash for years." Mama set her plate in the sink. "He doesn't mind the begging, Polly, so long as he isn't the one to do it."

TWENTY-TWO
Chauffeur Sam

Mama retired to her room in search of something suitable to wear. I headed outside. The screen door slammed behind me. Out on the porch, I dangled my legs between the rails. I kicked my heels, marking time. The wood made a satisfying *thump-thump-thump*. Where in the blazes was Daddy? Sleeping it off on some roadside, where any passerby could spot him and mutter, "Baxter trash"? Or dead in some ditch?

And what would happen if Meemaw didn't open her purse strings? Mama's paycheck couldn't be enough to live on, or we'd be living on it already.

Someone turned onto our street.

Please please please let it be Daddy.

Nope. Not a truck, but a regular old car.

"Sam's here," I called. Mama hadn't made it outside. She was still getting gussied up. "And Timbre Ann's with him." Even with the dust Sam's sedan kicked up, I could make out the shape of her head, braids and all.

Shoot, Mama hadn't told me Timbre Ann was getting to go. I couldn't let her witness a Baxter mercy mission. She already didn't like Daddy. Now she'd disapprove of him all the more.

"While I'm gone, don't stray far from the yard, Polly," Mama said, closing the front door and looking to me for outfit approval, something she did whenever we went to Meemaw's. First I'd look her over, and then she'd check my outfit.

I took her in from heel to head. She usually went around in bare feet and pedal pushers, but today she'd put on stockings, pumps, and a navy schoolmarm dress. There could only be one woman she was copying: Aunt Clara.

"Look at you," I said, disgusted. I pounded my heel harder.

"Careful, the last thing we need is for this porch to come falling down."

Sheesh. First she looked like a schoolteacher, now she sounded like one. I pulled my legs through the railings and blocked the stairs.

"How come Timbre Ann gets to go along for the ride and I don't?"

Mama clutched her pocketbook and looked out to where Sam stood by the driver's door. He waited for Mama like he was her chauffeur, taking his hat off and squinting into the sun.

"I suppose Sam brought Timbre Ann because it wouldn't look proper driving alone with me otherwise." Mama tilted her head to the sky, as if the puffy clouds held some answer for the ways of the world. I reckoned she didn't get the answer she wanted, because in a tired voice she added, "Fine. You can come. But when Sam drops us, stay out of sight. No need to hear a lecture about the evils of letting you wear cutoff dungarees, is there?"

"No, ma'am," I said. They weren't the exact words I wanted to hear, but at least I was getting to go.

TWENTY-THREE
White Lies

"Shoe shopping time." Timbre Ann hopped out of the front seat, ready to turn it over to Mama. She elbowed me. "If you want, you can have my old pair. Size seven should fit you, shouldn't it?"

"No need," Mama said. I hoped she was turning down Timbre Ann's shoe offer, but it was the front seat Mama declined. "The backseat is fine. Isn't it, Polly?"

"Fine by me," I said.

Timbre Ann crinkled her nose. Her code for asking what was up. I shrugged, a signal to Timbre Ann that meant "tell you later."

Even if I had the privacy to lean over and tell the gospel truth in Timbre Ann's ear, I wouldn't. The thought of her knowing I hated her hand-me-downs and that Daddy didn't come home made my insides itchy.

I scooched across the vinyl, wondering where Sam had stashed that pouch full of money. In the car? In a box buried in the woods? Where would it be safe? Nowhere the Sheriff would find it—that was for sure.

Mama slid in behind me and Sam pulled away from the curb. Off we went, the begging Baxters. Mama sat ramrod straight, like she was used to getting chauffeured around. She needn't have bothered. For once, Mrs. Busybody O'Brien was nowhere to be seen.

"Who's minding the shop?" I asked, thinking it better to ask questions than to be the one asked.

"Peter." Timbre Ann turned in her seat. "You remember him, don't you? We went to his family's store. Fulbright's."

"Sure." I hadn't forgotten Peter or the way he handed Timbre Ann her change.

"That boy is a born salesman," Sam said. "He sold five of my walking sticks for three dollars apiece."

Sam hit his blinker and turned on Old Holcolm Road, a longer route than cutting through downtown but one that was less likely to have much traffic. The last thing we needed was for Sheriff Wilkes to spot us. I could tell it was on Sam's mind, too. He kept an extra careful watch on the rearview mirror. I was sure he wanted no surprises. Whether Mama knew it or not, he was taking a big risk in driving us.

"Peter's the best," Timbre Ann said. "You know Pa's teaching him to tally the books, too."

"What a fine young man you have working for you."
Mama winked at me, as if to say, *Doesn't that beat all,
Timbre Ann has a schoolgirl crush.*

"Since when do boys come before books?" I asked,
all snotty. "Since you got your monthly?"

Timbre Ann whirled around so fast her braids hit her
cheeks. "Polly!"

"Polly Beatrice Baxter," Mama said. "Don't be
fresh."

"Sorry," I said. I wasn't sorry. Sam should know Timbre Ann liked a boy. An older boy.

"Don't listen to her, Pa," Timbre Ann said. "Polly
knows nothing. Peter and I are just friends."

"Polly knows plenty. So do you," Sam said, gruff-
like. "You know the rules—no dating until you are sixteen. And then only in groups. You got me?"

"Yessir," Timbre Ann said.

"Good."

I liked seeing Sam rule his roost, but a split second
later he chuckled. "Thanks for the warning, Polly. I reckon
I better carve a baseball bat to keep the boys away. My
daughter's got brains and beauty."

"Oh, Pa."

Leave it to Sam to not only *not* get mad, but to end up
complimenting Timbre Ann.

"Well," Mama said, "I'm glad you have Peter. I'd hate to think you closed shop to run us to Mother's. We do appreciate the ride."

"How come Mr. Baxter didn't take you? Is he working?" Timbre Ann asked, knowing full well he wasn't. She was trying to get back at me either for ratting out her crush on Peter or for having to carry us to Meemaw's in the first place. Well, it wouldn't work.

"Will be," I said. Usually I reserved my whoppers for commenting on Meemaw's appearance. "His truck broke down on the way to check out a job. Otherwise, he'd have been back to take us to Pine Bluff."

Mama quietly cleared her throat. I was pushing it.

"Can't Peter give Mr. Baxter a tow?" Timbre Ann asked.

Timbre Ann had backed me into a corner. Only Negroes went to Biggs Repair. Daddy would never go there.

"He's already gone to Teensy's," I said. That wasn't an out-and-out lie. That's the last place he was, playing poker in the back room. "He called us from there. He didn't want Mama and me to fret."

Mama squeezed my knee. I swallowed. I was trying her patience but good.

Timbre Ann upped the ante. "We can drop you at Teensy's." She was calling my bluff. "Can't we, Pa?"

"No," I said, louder than I meant to. A blotch climbed up my neck and onto my cheeks. It blared like a neon sign: POLLY BAXTER. LIAR. LIAR. LIAR! "Daddy's dirty from being stranded. Meemaw hates anything less than Sunday best."

"I understand," said Sam. "Man's in no mood to see the mother-in-law after he's spent time on the side of the road."

"Indeed," said Mama, drawing the conversation to a close.

An icy silence settled over us. I wished Sam had turned the radio on. If the top forty countdown had been playing, Mama and I could have treated them to a family sing-along. Our "Mack the Knife" was top-notch, almost as good as Bobby Darin's. Instead, I crossed and uncrossed my legs. My lies had me all fidgety. Mama shifted her pocketbook and poked me in the side.

"Knock it off," she whispered. "These folks are our friends."

TWENTY-FOUR
Last Trip

This trip to Meemaw's, I didn't have to worry about choosing which fork to use. Still, I was nauseous as we climbed her long, winding drive. Mama got all serious-like, too. She pulled a compact from her pocketbook; then, looking in the mirror, she dotted her hairline with a handkerchief, wiped away any sweat beads, and made sure not one of her auburn hairs had been mussed from its super-sprayed flip.

"Here's fine," said Mama, when we were halfway up Meemaw's steep drive. "Mother's not expecting me so early. I wouldn't want the car doors to wake her if she's resting."

Who did Mama think she was fooling? Meemaw would have a heart attack seeing Mama get dropped off by a Negro, knowing no way, no how, could she afford a driver.

Sam pulled into the brush. "Instead of idling here, I

think I'll take these two for a cold RC cola. They could use a cooling off."

"I'm not thirsty," Timbre Ann said.

"Me, neither."

"Didn't say you were," Sam said. "Said you could use a cooling off."

Mama clasped her pocketbook. "Where—where would . . ." She struggled for the right words as her hand tugged on the door handle.

"Not to worry. I know a bait shack not that far from here. We can get a soda there," Sam said, knowing we couldn't all be served together at Woolworth's or any other white-owned soda counter.

I was sure Mama was about to say yes. Instead, much to everyone's surprise, "Otis" escaped from her lips. Like in a horror movie, out of nowhere, Daddy's face framed Mama's window.

"Otis, gracious—you scared the dickens out of us!"

His truck was a ways ahead, the hood pointed in our direction. He must've pulled to the side when he saw Sam's car coming.

"Daddy!" I hopped out of the car. Grabbed him and hugged him hard. Thank heavens he was safe. "What are you doing here?"

"Seeing to things." He rubbed his red-rimmed eyes

and ushered Mama from the back seat. "I take it you heard, which is why you took a ride from these here fine folks."

I cringed. The way Daddy's lips tightened when calling them "fine folks" let everyone know what Daddy really thought of Sam and Timbre Ann.

Sam tossed a few ice cubes of his own in his usual sweet-tea voice. "Seeing that you've found a return ride, we'll be on our way." He tipped his hat. "Mrs. Baxter, Polly."

"Heard what? What's going on?" Mama asked, still standing in the path of the Biggses' car. Whatever had happened, I reckoned she didn't want Sam and Timbre Ann to leave until she'd heard what it was.

Daddy led Mama a few feet away. I followed.

"I was just headed home to tell you. It's bad, Lisbeth. Irma had a heart attack."

"What? When?" Mama muttered.

"Sometime after midnight. Clara called, looking for Jimmy. He was sitting in on our game. We came right over."

Uncle Jimmy playing poker? Since when were he and Daddy poker buddies?

"Why? Why didn't you call home and wake me?" Mama was close to tears.

"You'd been so sick. I thought it best you sleep." Daddy cupped her cheek. "There was nothing you could do, darling. You couldn't bring her back. No one could."

Bring her back? Meemaw was dead? Dead!

Mama dropped her pocketbook. Her lipstick rolled into the underbrush. She reached for me. I held her steady, worried that her pull, as strong as an undertow, would tug us under.

TWENTY-FIVE
Cracks

Holcolm County prided itself on two things: magnolia blossoms and the ability to toll the death knell before the *Holcolm Sentinel* obituary pages were typeset. The county didn't let Meemaw down. The moment we stepped foot in our door, the town busybodies started their condolence calling. The wall phone in the kitchen rang off the hook.

"Will you get that, Otis? I'm not feeling right. Dizzy," Mama said, placing her hand on the wall to steady herself.

"Sure, sweet thing, you go and rest." He kissed her forehead. "Polly and I'll hold down the fort."

When Mama had shut their bedroom door, he turned to me. "Take that blasted phone off the hook. That grandmother of yours did what she could to see this entire town treated us like trash."

I did as Daddy said. I, too, didn't feel like hearing any "Oh so sorry's" from a bunch of biddies who didn't know the kind of granny Meemaw was. Chastising me for not using the right fork. Wiping off my kisses. Trying to come between Mama and Daddy. Yessiree, no sugar sympathy calls for me. But what would we do about the front door? On television, as soon as someone died, folks dropped by with cakes and casseroles. Mama didn't look up to playing hostess, but I was. Surefire, we could use the food.

"Got to head into town," Daddy said, turning toward the back door. "Jimmy said he had a proposal for me. A business proposal."

First they played poker and now Jimmy was going to offer him a job? That didn't sound right. "But you keyed his car."

"Ah, he said my temper made me a man of action. And that's what he needed. A man of action."

Daddy dug in his front pocket and palmed his truck keys. He tossed them in the air, happy as all get out.

"Aww, Polly, don't be like that," Daddy said. He lifted my chin, tried to butter me up. "Like me, Jimmy ain't a Pritchard. No reason we should be enemies."

"True enough," I said, but I wasn't so sure.

"Now, don't let your mama lift a finger until I get back. Okay, Polly-gal?" He grabbed the brim of his ball cap and resettled it low over his eyes before heading out. "Fix her whatever she wants for supper."

"But there's nothing to eat."

He stopped, caught between me and the back door. "What?"

"Mama gave most of the coffee can money to the Sheriff. But where's the rest of it?"

Under his ball cap, Daddy's eyes narrowed. "Sheriff Wilkes came by?"

I bit my lip. Mama hadn't told him?

"When?" Daddy asked. "When was the Sheriff here?"

"Awhile ago. Aunt Clara sent him. To pay for a new paint job."

"How much did Lisbeth give him?"

I cringed. "Forty-three dollars."

Daddy's eyes grew steely. "Where would she get that kind of cash? Not from that damn coffee can."

I didn't have an answer. Not one I could give. Mama hadn't told me a thing. If she didn't get that money from the coffee can, where did she get it?

He pounded his fist in his palm, like a pitcher ready to throw a red-hot strike. "Lisbeth!" he called down the hallway.

"Don't, Daddy. Let her sleep." I needed to calm him quick. "I bet it was Meemaw's fault. Bet she told Mama to sock money away. For a rainy day or something."

He turned. "Think so?"

"Know so," I said.

He cocked his head, thinking it over. He knelt beside my chair. "Reckon you're right, Polly-gal."

I thought he might ruffle my hair, his way of saying sorry, but he didn't. "Despite the Battle-Ax planting thoughts in your mama's head, I don't plan to let my family go hungry. Never have. Never will," he said.

I nodded. That was true. I suppose money had been tight plenty of times, and we had never, not once, starved.

"Whatever job Jimmy is offering, I'll take it. In fact, I'll get him to front me some cash tonight and will make a run to the grocery, all right?"

He smoothed back my bangs. Looked hard into my eyes. Mama was wrong. Daddy wasn't above begging. That's what taking a job from Uncle Jimmy would be. Begging.

"Irma kicked us around, but it was your mama that always went back for more. Don't know why, but she loved that woman."

"Yessir, she did." I wondered how Mama could muster up love for a woman who made her life plenty miserable.

"And the damn Battle-Ax didn't do a thing to deserve it." Gently, Daddy took me by the shoulders. "Now that Irma ain't here, things will be better, I swear."

"Sure," I said, not so sure Daddy would, or could, keep his word.

"Pinky swear, all right?"

I looped my finger through his, and he pulled me in for a hug. Shucks, I realized, burying my nose in his neck and smelling his sweaty smell, maybe Mama couldn't help but love Meemaw. Love was like that. Like a crack creeping up a dam. No matter how high the walls, a few drops could spill out. And if you weren't careful, a steady stream could fill you to the brim.

TWENTY-SIX
Condolence Call

From the front porch, I watched Daddy go. Normally he would've cranked the radio in search of Johnny Cash or Elvis—his two-head-to-toe black-wearing, bad-boy heroes—but probably to keep from waking Mama, he didn't touch the dashboard dial. He popped the truck into neutral and it slid silently down the drive. He better come back with a bag of groceries. More and more I felt divided into two Pollys—the one that believed Daddy could do no wrong, and the one that believed Daddy could do no right. The jury was still out on which one would win.

When he was gone, I headed inside to survey the cleaning that needed to be done. Folks on Chessup Street weren't exactly friendly—at least not with us Baxters—but bad news could build bridges.

I imagined a big old bridge made out of ham bake (egg noodles, scraps of ham and cheese, and mushroom soup) along with Hawaiian salad (fruit cocktail mixed with whipped cream and those teeny tiny marshmallows), leading from the neighbors' closed doors to ours. A table of food in honor of Meemaw meeting her Maker suited me fine.

I got to work, gathering the newspapers that Daddy left at the foot of his armchair. Inside the stack I found an empty Jack Daniel's bottle. Under the couch I found another, though it wasn't all the way empty.

I snuck a sip. It burned. I made myself swallow. I thought I might heave, right there on the throw rug.

"Yuck."

I poured what little was left down the drain. Did Daddy actually like this stuff? It tasted terrible. Like pure spite. No wonder Mama called it the devil's drink.

I stuffed the bottles in the trash and hauled the garbage to the cans out back, under my window. Then I went around front to hunt for a good stick to whack the throw rugs. I beat those dusty old things until my arm was as sore as a baseball pitcher who'd gone into overtime.

When that was done, I poured myself a glass of sweet tea, which didn't fully take away the icky whiskey taste, but at least it cured my thirst.

With nothing left to do, I sat vigil on the sofa.

The minute hand moved at a snail's pace until sixty had passed. It took me over an hour to clean, and by now another hour was up. And that was plenty long enough to toss together a casserole. Mama had baked Mrs. O'Brien a batch of sugar cookies when her dog, Duke, got run over, and no one even liked that mangy mutt. Least she could have done was return the gesture.

Then it hit me. Nobody was coming. Nobody.

I stomped into the kitchen, opening and closing cabinets in search of something edible. Not ten yards away, Mrs. O'Brien crouched, pulling weeds from her garden. She nodded her head, curt-like, enough to show she saw me, but not enough to be considered a pleasantry. I chewed my anger like a wad of gum. And it wasn't only Mrs. O'Brien that had me riled. It was Daddy, too. Leaving me to string together a meal for Mama out of a can of beets and a few slices of store-bought bread.

Well, it would have to do.

I was getting out the can opener—the handheld twisty kind, not the fancy electric counter contraption Aunt Clara owned—when I heard footsteps lumber up the back porch. I could smell the fortifying goodness of a warm and crispy casserole. Ha! I'd tossed my faith in the fire a minute too soon.

"Do you need some muscle to help you work that thing?"

Henri? Lordy Lou, what was she doing here?

"Pleased to see you, too," she said, reading the none-to-happy look on my face.

"Sorry, c'mon in. Surprised is all," I said. I hopped off the kitchen chair, the can opener still halfway attached to the lid, and ushered Henri in. Let Mrs. O'Brien gossip. As long as she didn't ring the Sheriff, who was going to care? Not me.

Whatever Henri carried between those two pot holders smelled mighty good. It distracted me so much that I almost missed Timbre Ann sliding in behind her, carrying a pineapple upside-down cake. My favorite.

I rushed around, shutting the empty and open cabinets right quick.

"Daddy's gone to get groceries," I said, thankful I'd had the sense to hide his empty bottles in the trash. "Mama's asleep."

"Not with all of your noise, little miss." Mama staggered into the room. She wore her cotton gown, her hair a mess of bird's-nest knots. "Oh, Henri, you shouldn't have," she said when she saw the food they carried.

"Nonsense." Henri elbowed the beets out of her way and laid the casserole on the counter. "Lisbeth, I know how heavy your heart is. She may not have been the best mama, but she was the only mama you had." Pot holders still gripped in each hand, she hugged Mama hard.

It only took a second for Mama to be wrapped in Henri's arms before she gave way to a fit of tears. Her nose scrunched, her face turned as bright as those beets, and in between heaves of her chest, she managed to push out a string of words. "She never loved me. Never."

"Hush, don't say that." Henri patted Mama's back, moving her hand in slow, comforting circles.

"Well, she never forgave me. That much is true. Me. Pregnant at fifteen."

Over Mama's shoulders, Henri nodded to Timbre Ann and me. A request to go on and get. To leave the two of them alone. That we needn't bear witness to Mama's grief.

I didn't have to be told twice. I ran out the back door and into the woods, not once checking to see if Timbre Ann followed suit. I could hear her calling after me.

"Polly, wait up!" she hollered, but all I could hear were Mama's words: "Pregnant at fifteen."

Meemaw never forgave Mama for having me. Me.

TWENTY-SEVEN
Lightning Quick

Hand over fist, I climbed an elm. The bark cut into my palms, but I didn't care. It hurt, but everything hurt. My side ached from running full sprint. My shin pained from when I'd lost my footing and hit the tree. I hadn't noticed the blood that beaded and trailed down my leg. Now there was no way I could miss it. To stay hidden, I crouched with my knees to my chest, like the duck-and-cover position we practiced at school in case the Russians attacked.

I could see Timbre Ann a ways away. She stopped to catch her breath. I held mine.

"Wait up, wait for me."

Timbre Ann darted through the pines, favoring her side. She looked to have gotten a side cramp. Or maybe her monthly had come early.

Having caught her breath, she called, "Polly, don't fret. All mamas-to-be act like that. It's the hormones."

Mamas to be? Mama was having a baby? *My* mama?

I had to stop myself from jumping out of that tree. Because if I did, I'd lightning quick wrestle her to the ground. *You think you're so smart, don't you?* I thought. *You think you have to tell me my mama's pregnant? I've known all along. Just didn't choose to share it with you!*

Timbre Ann kept running towards home. As much as I wanted to run after her, I stayed put. Another white lie would do me no good.

TWENTY-EIGHT
Keeping Count

Timbre Ann circled back. I stayed stock-still and tried
to blend in with the trees. If I could stop panting like a dog,
she might not spot me. To keep quiet, I counted. Silently.

One Mississippi, two Mississippi . . . By the time I
reached two hundred and seventy-five, she turned tail,
calling, "Forget you, Polly Baxter. I'm too old to play
hide-and-seek."

Let her tattle on me. Tell Mama I was missing. Would
serve Mama right—choosing to tell the Biggses about the
baby and not me. No way, no how, was I following Timbre Ann home. What did I have to go home to—Mama
keeping secrets, a sliver of cold casserole, and watching
the window for Daddy?

When I was sure Timbre Ann had truly left and was-
n't somewhere spying on me, I stretched out of my pret-
zel position. My lungs finally stopped their jackhammer
pounding, but my thoughts didn't. I kept counting—no
longer to keep quiet, but to get quiet.

Counting was a trick Mama'd taught me. Whenever I had trouble sleeping, Mama would impersonate Granddaddy Pritchard. "Try counting, little miss," she'd say, sticking out her gut like her daddy must have. "Not sheep but plain old numbers. If you make it to one thousand and thirty-three and your mind hasn't stopped chasing its tail, my name is not Alabaster Alexander Pritchard."

But today I had more cares than I could count. Timbre Ann. Mama. Daddy. The baby. Shoot, once I wanted a Betsy Wetsy, and all I got was a sewing scrap doll. If Mama and Daddy couldn't afford a store-bought baby, how could they afford a real one?

I scanned the nearby trees, searching for nests. There were none. The wind rustled the leaves, but I didn't hear one twitter. I could've used a friend right then. Heck, if I couldn't find a bird, a baby might fit the bill. A baby didn't talk, didn't stick its nose where it wasn't wanted, didn't make you feel bad. A baby didn't do anything but sleep, cry, pee, and poop. That I could handle.

Baby Baxter would need me to teach it a trick or two. A magic trick to wipe the worries away. Instead of singing a lullaby, I'd count the baby to sleep. One Mississippi, two Mississippi . . .

TWENTY-NINE
Help

Dusk had settled in, blanketing the woods in long shadows. It was way past dark. I wanted my bed. My warm bed. My cotton pajamas, the ones with the worn lace around the neck and underarms. A hand-me-down from Mama, not from Timbre Ann.

I shimmied from the branch and hugged the bark, trying to climb down. The moon gave off a bit of light, but not enough to see the handholds I'd found so easily in the daylight. I slipped. Slipped some more. The bark skinned my hand and I couldn't hold on. I fell, hit the ground. All my weight slammed on my ankle.

"Tarnation." I curled into a ball at the base of the tree. I'd done it now. Tears sprung to my eyes. My ankle hurt like the dickens.

I forced myself onto my palms, my knees, my feet. I took one step. Two. It hurt bad, too bad. No way could I make it home. I threw a handful of pine straw.

"Help! Daddy! Mama! Please . . ." I sucked in my tears and screamed again. "Please, please, I'm out here. Find me!"

Nothing. An owl hooted. Something—a squirrel, a fox—ran in the brush. I shivered, scooting as fast as I could back to the base of the tree. Then I hugged my knees to my chest and let the tears fall.

THIRTY
Piggyback

Daddy found me. I didn't hear him call me, though his voice had worn raspy from hollering my name. I'd fallen asleep. All cried out—tired out—at the base of that tree. He woke me, pulling me to him before I was even sure he was real, that he was really there.

"Polly-gal, you scared me. Scared me to death!" He rocked me back and forth. "Are you all right? What happened?"

I pointed to the tree. I bit my lip. "I fell. Hurt my ankle."

"It's all right now. Daddy's here." He crouched down for a look. In the faint moonlight, all we could see was that my ankle had swelled up big. "That doesn't look good. We better get you home."

He tried to lift me, but from the forest floor, I was too heavy. Deadweight.

"How about a piggyback ride?" Daddy asked. He led

me to a stump and helped me climb on up. "Less likely to bang your foot that way."

Daddy took my legs, careful not to bump my swollen ankle, and wrapped each one around his middle. He groaned under my weight. I wasn't an itty-bitty thing anymore. As he shifted me, I tossed my arms around his neck like a noose. I hadn't ridden piggyback since-shoot, I couldn't remember when.

"I've been hunting these woods almost an hour. I was all set to call the Sheriff."

"Really?"

The thought of beady-eyed Sheriff Wilkes out here scouring the woods gave me the heebie-jeebies, but I liked knowing Mama and Daddy were worried sick, almost organizing a search party. That's what Ward and June Cleaver would do if Wally or the Beav didn't make it home by sundown. Sam and Henri, too, if Timbre Ann ever went missing. Not that she ever would.

"What got into you? It ain't like you to run off."

"I'm a Baxter, ain't I," I said, full of piss and vinegar. "I reckon the apple don't fall far from the tree."

"And being a Baxter is such a bad thing?" Daddy asked.

I laid my chin on his shoulder. "Sometimes."

"Gospel truth?" He craned his neck and caught my eye.

I reckoned he didn't want me to lie.

"Lots of times," I said.

Daddy sighed; his breath rose and fell with his footsteps. "Well, it's been a hard day. Harder than most. Irma passing. Your mother grieving."

I was more upset about the baby. About Mama and Daddy keeping it from me, but maybe he was right. If Timbre Ann's granny died, she'd let the waterworks flow. No problem. And here I was, Polly Beatrice Hooligan Baxter, not shedding a tear.

"Isn't it wrong not to be tore up when someone dies?"

"Why, you'd miss most folks, wouldn't you? You'd miss your Mama. You'd miss me."

I slipped some and Daddy hiked me higher.

"'Course,'" I said, shivering at the thought of Mama or Daddy being dead and gone. Of anyone that close to me dying. Even Big Mouth Timbre Ann, who I never wanted to see again.

"See, there ain't nothing wrong with you," Daddy said. "That seesaw feeling comes with the territory when someone you wanted to love — but didn't — dies."

"Oh." I wondered if that seesaw feeling Daddy spoke of was the same as the flip-flopping my gut often did over him. Could that be A-okay, too?

We walked on. The moon followed us, dodging in and

out of the pines, bathing the woods in a silvery glow. It was so quiet I could hear the *swish, swish, swish,* of Daddy's jeans rubbing as he walked. That, coupled with the chirping crickets, reminded me of the one-two-three of a slow country waltz. I liked the idea of that—our night-time piggyback ride a kind of father-daughter dance.

My gut rumbled. It broke our dancing spell.

"You hungry, Polly-gal?"

"Yessir." I'd never gotten any of Henri's casserole.

"Good. Your mama should have a pan of steak and onions waiting on us."

"Steak and onions?"

"When did you get to be such a penny pincher?" He decoded my cash-register tone. "Told you I'd get Jimmy to spot me some cash. Don't worry. I didn't blow it all on steak and onions. I got milk. Cheese. Bologna. We've got a full fridge."

At the edge of woods, Daddy stopped and gingerly sat me on a stump. "Now, let me see how that foot of yours is doing."

Daddy got on his knees for a closer look.

My foot hurt plenty. What hurt more though was a strange stinging right behind my eyes. Like I might cry from Daddy doing everything a daddy should do.

He loosened my laces. Eased off my shoe, just as I

had his work boot that night he was too drunk to manage on his own. I bit my lip.

"Don't cry, Polly-gal." His words said to buck up, but he soon added, "Let it out, let it all out."

I squeezed shut my eyes.

"What is it? It's okay. You're okay."

"How come . . . how come . . ."

"Go ahead. Spit it out."

"How come you can't always act this way?"

Daddy lifted my chin. His thumb smudged the wet streaks trailing my cheeks. "And what way is that?"

"Like now. Like a television daddy. Doing and saying everything right."

"A television daddy, huh?"

"Yeah," I said. I didn't care if I sounded silly. Like a little kid. "You do plenty of things better than . . . than Beaver's daddy." I caught myself. I almost said Timbre Ann's daddy. Better than Sam. "Flip flapjacks, play catch, sing radio songs. But you haven't done any of that. Not since . . ." I didn't want to say it. "Since you lost your job."

"My job, huh?"

"Which was when you started . . . started drinking," I said, my tongue heavy.

Not far away, somebody's porch light flickered on. In its glow, I could see Daddy's face. It looked worn, worried.

"All my life I've been told I was a disappointment. My father. Your grandmother. Now you."

"I didn't say that, Daddy. I didn't."

"Don't interrupt. You asked a question—hard as it was to hear—and you deserve an answer." Daddy rubbed his face, jamming his fists into his eyes. When he removed them I could tell he'd been crying.

I touched his cheeks. They were wet, just like mine.

"I got my faults, Polly-gal. But I promise you—" Daddy cleared his throat. He took my hand. "I'll get a job, and on top of that, no more drinking. Not a drop. If it takes becoming a teetotaler to be a better father, I aim to do it."

" 'Cause of the baby?" I asked, jealous of that little life growing inside Mama.

Daddy stood. Stock-still, he didn't say a word. As quiet as it was out there in the woods, I wasn't sure he'd heard me.

"No, Polly-gal, not because of the baby. Because of you." He dug a tin of chewing tobacco out of his back pocket and stuck a wad in his mouth. His bottom lip stuck out so far, he could've been pouting. "Now, let's get you home, fed, and to bed. It's been a helluva day."

THIRTY-ONE
Between Us Baxters

Barefoot, Mama ran into the yard. She must've been keeping one eye on the back door and one eye on the supper she kept warming on the stove. She left the door open and that steak-and-onions smell coming from inside set my stomach to rumbling.

"Goodness, I thought you'd be back hours ago," Mama said, when she saw Daddy cradle-carrying me, like he did when I was little and had fallen asleep on the floor. "I was right to worry, my baby's hurt. What happened?"

Her fingers tugged at a piece of pine straw that caught in my hair. She kissed my face all over. Lips, cheeks, nose, and each eyelid.

"She'll survive. Twisted ankle is all."

Daddy climbed the porch stairs and carried me into the living room.

"It hurts bad. Real bad," I said, pleased as punch at all the attention I was getting. I'd played my last sympathy card, though. Now that Mama saw I wasn't on death's door, she lit into me. Her hands flew to her hips.

"Polly Beatrice Baxter, running out like that and not coming home by dark, why you about gave me a heart attack." A moment too late, she realized what she said, and shook her head, erasing the thought. "Gracious, I didn't mean that."

"Sorry, Mama. I didn't mean to scare you."

She smoothed my ruffled hair. "Of course you didn't." Mama kissed me again and plumped up a threadbare throw pillow. "Lay her here, on the sofa. I'll get ice for her foot."

She continued to bustle around, doing ten things at once. She filled the dish towel that hung over her shoulder with ice cubes, grabbed herself another towel, set up television trays, and dished out plates.

"Rang Clara when I couldn't find you," Mama said, from the kitchen.

"Oh, Mama. Why?"

"Thought you might have gone there, the one place we'd be sure not to look. Wouldn't you know she gave me an earful, unable to keep tabs on my own daughter? I could kick myself for calling her."

Mama served Daddy and then me. I dug in, cutting the meat in large chunks. I didn't care that it was overcooked, not one bit of juice running onto the plate. Daddy bought it, Mama fixed it, and I aimed to eat it.

"She made all the funeral arrangements without me," Mama said, again from the kitchen. "Flowers, casket, even what dress to bury Mother in. The service is Wednesday. Otis, do you think the suit you wore for my father's funeral still fits?"

"If it doesn't, I'll get a new one."

"We can't afford a new one. I'll let the seams out if need be."

"I'll get a new one," Daddy said, firm-like. "I'm doing some work for Jimmy now. He paid me some money up front. A lump sum. I can afford me a new suit."

"Hear, hear. A job." I raised my glass. No one toasted but me. I put my milk down on the television tray without drinking any.

Mama came back empty-handed. "A job with Jimmy?"

"Yeah, a job. And don't you go bad-mouthing it. It pays more than the mill." Daddy took a bite of steak, chewed, then swallowed.

"But . . ." Mama grabbed at the daisy-covered dish towel stuck in her apron. She wound it around and around her wrist. "Otis, I don't like the sound of this. Jimmy and Clara, they're our family, but they're not our friends."

"Are now. Now that I told them you and Polly here would stop seeing the Biggses."

"You did what?" Mama whipped that towel fast. It made a soft whoosh—not a cracking sound. "How could you?"

"Listen, Lisbeth, like it or not, things are heating up." Daddy got up from his chair. "My only aim is to keep this family safe."

"But, Otis," Mama said. "I depend on Henri. I depend on Sam."

"Well, now you can start depending on me, all right?"

Mama shivered, as if she'd gotten a sudden chill. Why didn't Daddy tell her? Tell her what he told me? As much as I didn't like the idea of not seeing Sam and Henri, I was glad not to have to see Timbre Ann. I didn't want to see her know-it-all face. Not now, not ever. Mama should know—know what Daddy promised. Knowing that might make giving up the Biggses worth it.

"Mama, Daddy's not drinking anymore. Not one drop." There, that was all the convincing she'd need.

"Is that what you told her?" Mama asked.

"Damn straight." Daddy dug in his jacket pocket and handed Mama a silver flask.

"AAP," she said, reading the engraved initials. "This was my father's. He gave you this?"

"He gave it to me the day Polly was born." He crinkled his face the way I had when I sipped from his whiskey bottle. "I reckon he didn't mean for me to use it to go on a bender, but when I lost that job I just . . ." Daddy trailed off. He wrapped his fingers around Mama's. "In any case, it's best you hold on to it."

Mama stared at the silver flask. "Otis, I want to believe you. I want to." Mama blinked. She was getting teary eyed. "But Mother never stopped. She never did. I know her heart gave out, but that liquor—that's what did her in."

Mama broke down. Her shoulders shook, the same way as they had with Henri.

"Don't cry, darling." Daddy wrapped her in his arms. He held her like that, like a wounded bird, until her tears stopped.

"Here, Mama," I said, "come sit by me."

Daddy sat her next to me. He set her up a television tray. Then he went to the kitchen. Went and got her plate.

"You best eat now, Lisbeth. Protein is good for the baby."

"Baby?" She shot him a look that said, *Why are you talking about this in front of Polly?*

"Oh, don't worry, Polly knows." Daddy set her plate on the empty television tray. "She didn't mind at all it took this long *for her* to find out." The way Daddy said it didn't sound like he was talking about me. It sounded like he was talking about him.

"Didn't mind at all? Is that so?" I'd heard them fight enough to know that Mama's voice was full of the unsaid.

My gut tightened. They were talking in code. Did that mean . . . ? No, it couldn't. Daddy couldn't have learned about the baby from me?

"If Polly forgave me, she'll forgive you," Daddy said, holding out his no-drinking-promise like a white flag.

"I already forgive you, Mama." If I did, maybe Daddy would, too. I held out my hand. Made her take it. Why wouldn't she . . . why wouldn't she have told him?

"Thanks, sweetie." She moved the ice pack back onto my ankle. I hadn't felt it slip off. I'd gone numb inside and out. Pins and needles, but not in my ankle, in my chest. Surely, Mama had to have planned on telling us together, both Daddy and me. Heck, Timbre Ann had ruined our special moment. This was her fault. Not Daddy's.

"I am sorry you found out this way. I should have told you myself." Mama stared at her fingernails, all bit up like mine. "A baby means big changes for us all. Why, I needed some time to get used to the idea myself. That's why I didn't tell you."

She gave my knee a pat, a love pat, but her eyes stayed locked with Daddy's. Though we weren't sitting in the truck, I was stuck in the middle again. They weren't talking about me so much as through me. "You can understand that, can't you, Polly?"

I glanced at Daddy. He arched his eyebrow, giving me the go-ahead, as he returned to his supper. "Sure, Mama, but you could have told me. I'm happy about the baby."

"You are?" Mama sounded surprised.

"We all are," Daddy said. He worked a fatty spot in his steak, his knife scratching his plate, making that nail-on-the-chalkboard sound that gave me the heebie-jeebies.

"Now, family is family. No more secrets between us Baxters. Got that?"

We didn't nod, or say "Yessir," but Mama and me, we didn't disagree.

THIRTY-TWO
Wanted

In the middle of the night, my throbbing ankle woke me. Mama was there. Sitting in the old rocker that we'd patched last year by gluing a piece of plywood from the mill to the wicker seat to keep our butts from falling through. She had a ball of yarn in her lap and her knitting needles.

"Oh, baby," she said. "Does it hurt?"

I nodded. She went off to the bathroom and brought me back a glass of water and an aspirin.

"Here." She helped me hold the glass to my lips. Even though I could do it myself, I let her.

"Now, if that swelling isn't better by morning," Mama said, "you're going to the doctor. We've got to be sure it's not fractured or something. All right?"

"Sure, Mama." I didn't want to go to the doctor, but all her fussing pleased me plenty.

"Drink up."

I drank the rest of the water. She took the glass, setting it on my milk-crate nightstand. "Now, let's get you tucked in." She scooped my hair from my neck and spread it out over my pillow. She unfurled the thin blanket at the foot of my bed. It was still early October; the leaves wouldn't change until closer to Halloween. But, the evenings had finally grown chilly.

"Sleep tight, don't let the bedbugs bite," she said when she finished tucking me in.

I caught her hand as she got up to go. She sat back down, the bed creaking under her weight. I thought of my nests, all three of them: one each for Daddy, Mama, and me, tucked away in my dresser drawer. Mama hadn't been tucking nests away. Like Sam, she'd been tucking away money.

"What is it, honey?" she asked, reading the worry on my face. "Is it the baby? I told you I'm sorry for keeping that a secret."

"No, that's not it, Mama. Why were you saving that money?" She hadn't been planning on leaving—making us leave Daddy, had she? If he didn't stop his drinking?

"What money?"

"The money you gave the Sheriff?"

"That's not for you to worry about." She kissed my forehead and smoothed my wrinkled brow. "You're too young to be fretting about such grown-up stuff."

I propped up on my elbow. "I'm going to be a big sister. I'm getting grown."

"That you are. Now, get some good sleep." She laid me back down. "We'll see how that ankle is doing in the morning."

I swatted the bed. I should've figured she wouldn't tell me. I tried one last time.

"Mama, I believe him. I know you don't, but I do."

"Oh, Polly, we have to wait and see. That kind of promise can be hard to keep, even for a daddy who loves his daughter as much as your daddy loves you." Mama's fingers nipped at my chin. She gave it a tweak, making me grin if even just the slightest bit. "I'll tell you one thing though. I believe *in* him. I wouldn't have married him otherwise."

"Really?" I asked. Since he lost his job, it had seemed just the opposite—that she was waiting for him to screw up.

"Cross my heart and hope to die. Stick a needle in my eye," Mama said, repeating what she always heard Timbre Ann and me recite to each other as she got up to go.

In the sliver of light from the hallway, Mama looked like an angel of mercy. Like the one that might've been escorting Meemaw on up to heaven. Even as mean as she was, I reckoned that's where Meemaw was headed. Henri always said God loves drunkards and sinners most of all. For Meemaw's sake, I hoped that was true.

Mama hovered in the doorway. "You heard me today, didn't you? Is that why you ran off?"

"Yes, ma'am." My eyelids felt heavy. Drowsy. I closed my eyes and saw her sprouting angel wings.

"I am so sorry about that," she said, softly. "Your daddy and I had you young. That's true. But if hearing that made you think you weren't wanted, it's not the case. You were. You were wanted by both your daddy and me."

As she closed the door, that sliver of light disappeared, but the wings stayed, except now they were on my back, and they had me floating. "Wanted," I whispered, falling off to sleep.

THIRTY-THREE
Shopping Spree

Daddy rapped his knuckles on my door. "Leaving now, Polly-gal. Suit shopping. Let's go."

"Coming," I said. Earlier that morning, he and Mama had taken me to the doctor, like Mama said they would if the swelling didn't go down. The doctor had sent us to the hospital for X-rays. My ankle was a bluish purple and swollen to the size of a small watermelon, but it wasn't fractured like Mama feared. While we were at Holcolm Memorial, she'd made appointments for her first series of pregnancy checkups. "By my figuring," I'd heard her tell the nurse, "I'm about nine weeks along."

Daddy looked upward, counting back in his head. Nine weeks ago was before he got fired from the mill. Before he'd started drinking.

He pulled Mama to the side. "I reckon you had reason to keep the baby to yourself, Lisbeth," he whispered. "But no more drinking. I made Polly a promise. You can count on that. No more."

Leaning on the wall, trying to keep my balance on my bandaged ankle, I smiled, feeling as if I had just witnessed the Second Coming. They were both trying, and without any spill-my-milk-and-fall-on-the-floor prompting from me.

And now here Mama was, walking us to the front door and kissing us good-bye—me on the forehead and Daddy on the cheek.

"Get a nice suit now, Otis. In navy or black. Not brown. Clara will have a fit if you show up in brown."

Daddy winked at me. "Yes, dear," he said. I couldn't help but smile. He sounded just like Ward talking to June.

On the drive downtown, Daddy tuned the radio to WKTO. No music was playing, just a commercial. When the spot ended, the deejay came on.

"Last night, Johnson's Funeral Home, the only Negro funeral parlor in Holcolm County, had its back porch burnt down. The fire was caught before it spread to the main hall and Johnson's remains open for business."

Daddy clicked off the radio.

"But Daddy, I want to hear if they caught who did it." I reached to turn it back on, but Daddy grabbed my hand and started singing.

I kept thinking about that fire—about how Timbre Ann may have taken the news—but I joined in. "Mack the Knife" was my favorite song.

Once downtown, we parked on Magnolia. Daddy handed me a nickel and let me turn the dial on the parking meter. We'd paid for a good sixty minutes—plenty of time to find Daddy a suit.

"Steady now," Daddy said. He helped me up the curb to the sidewalk. I was fine hobbling on my own, but I still held on to his arm until we were inside the suit shop.

The bell above the door jingled as we entered. A few customers milled around.

"One moment. I'll be right with you."

There was no one I recognized in the store, save for Mr. Matthews, the store manager, taking pins out of a man's dress shirt. He had his back to us. He finished what he was doing before he whirled around. "Oh, hello," he said, his voice a lot less chipper. "I suppose you're here to purchase something for Mrs. Pritchard's funeral."

"Yessir, we are," I said. Mr. Matthews was a member of Grover Street Baptist, Meemaw's church. I reckoned he'd be at the service, frowning at us Baxters like the rest of the congregation.

"Well, let me show you our selection of suit coats. They will look fine with a pair of dark dungarees."

"I need a black suit. Like that one." Daddy pointed to a mannequin. "And some shiny shoes. And a fedora."

"That's some shopping spree," said Mr. Matthews.

"Don't you worry," Daddy said. "We're paying cash."

Lickety-split, Mr. Matthews got to work, showing Daddy suits and shoes, one after the other. When Daddy came out of the dressing room, he looked like a brand-new man. Mr. Matthews got out his tape measure and made sure Daddy's shoulder seams and such were just right. "It's the fit that makes the man," he said.

"That so? Well, then let's make sure I'm tailored to a T."

While Mr. Matthews made chalk marks on Daddy's new pinstripe suit, I wandered over to the belts. I fingered a few. The leather was sturdy but soft to the touch, like Meemaw's wrinkled cheek. The buckles sure were shiny though. I left my fingerprints all over one. I grabbed a hanky from the stack on display, a real handsome one, the same light blue as Daddy's eyes. I breathed on the buckle, and then polished it something fierce, wiping the smudges off.

"What are you doing, young lady?" Mr. Matthews's tone was downright displeased. A man in the back looked to see who he could be chastising.

"Sorry," I said, "I meant no harm."

He took the hanky out of my hand. "This linen is from England. It's meant to be folded like this"—with a flick of his wrists he made a nice, neat triangle—"and kept in the breast pocket." He stuffed it in a mannequin's pocket. It didn't fit quite right. It looked a little puffy instead of lying flat like it had been pressed with an iron, like all the others.

"When done right, it is a statement that says, 'Southern gentleman.' "

Behind Mr. Matthews's back, Daddy mouthed, "Well, la-di-da." I had to bite my cheek to keep from laughing.

"Now, who is going to buy this wrinkly mess?"

Daddy came to my rescue. "Thought hankies were for blowing your nose." He grabbed it from the mannequin's pocket. He winked at me. "Or your lady's nose." He held it to mine, and, going along with his joke—*ah . . . ah . . . achoo*—I pretended to sneeze.

Mr. Matthews clutched at his heart, just like they do in the movies. Surefire, I thought he was going to faint.

"That is not a toy." Mr. Matthews grabbed it back. "It's priced at three whole dollars, the most expensive handkerchief in the store, and just look at it. There is no way I can sell it now."

"I'll work it off somehow. After school and on weekends. Sweeping or stocking or something. I can even press shirts. I'm good with an iron."

Daddy and Mr. Matthews ignored my rattling on. They were in a staring contest—a pissing contest, Daddy would call it. Mr. Matthews sure acted like a sissy, but there was no way Daddy could win this one.

That is, until slowly he peeled off a five and laid it smack on the counter.

"I think that will cover it," he said. "Now, are you going to tally the rest of our bill, or what?"

THIRTY-FOUR
Well, Well

While Mr. Matthews got busy hemming Daddy's pants, we went over to Caroline's Creations, the store where Sally Jean had seen Timbre Ann shopping. I took a good long look through the picture window, making sure that neither my old enemy, nor my new one, was inside.

"I don't want you batting an eye at a price tag. You go pick yourself out whatever you want, and it doesn't have to be black," Daddy said, making his way to the ladies' scarves. "I'll be over here, getting a surprise for your mama."

Goosebumps sprang up on my arm. There were so many dresses to choose from. Ones with Peter Pan collars, belted ones with pencil skirts, A-lines, and in all the colors of the rainbow. No one would say I was much for fashion, but after wearing Timbre Ann's hand-me-downs for years, I felt as if I'd been let loose in a candy store.

It was some time before I spotted the one I wanted. A

dark green dress, the color of the Georgia pines. Golly, it was pretty, but when I saw the white eyelet flowers, sprinkled the way they were about the soft folds of the skirt, my sweet tooth got to aching.

"This one, Daddy," I said, taking it over to him. "This is the one that I want." It was just the kind of dress Meemaw would have wanted to see me in, but it'd be worth it to hear Mama suck in her breath and say, "Look at my daughter, soon to be a little woman."

"Go try it on. Make sure it fits," Daddy said, turning back to the scarves. He nodded at the saleswoman, who had been busy helping an elderly lady out onto the street.

I drew the maroon curtain closed. Once I got the dress over my head and gave it a tug, I saw that it fit nice around the middle and flared out a bit over my knees. The girl in the mirror may have looked twelve going on thirteen, but inside I felt fourteen going on forty, like know-it-all Timbre Ann.

Oh, how I wished she were here. I knew it wasn't nice, but part of me wanted to spin circles around her. "Naa-naa, I no longer need your colored castoffs."

When I came out, Daddy was gone. I hadn't meant to take so long. Where could he be? The men's room? This was a lady's shop—did they even have one? Lordy Lou, he hadn't gotten kicked out, had he?

"Don't fret, honey. Your father already paid for your dress and these scarves," said the sales lady. She had to be Miss Caroline, the owner. She didn't wear a name tag, but she spoke with authority. "He went to put more change in the meter. Now, let me just wrap this up for you." Her red fingernails clutched at my dress, but I hugged it to me, not wanting to hand it over until I had to.

At the register, she wrapped it up nice and neat in crinkly tissue paper, and when it was all done, she handed me a fancy bag with big fat cursive writing on the front. I didn't even bother with a "Thank you," not even as she chimed, "Come, again."

I spotted Daddy at the truck, smoking a cigarette. His back was to me, blocking out whatever poker buddy he had run into. The wind blew something fierce, catching my Caroline's Creations bag, and almost knocking me off my swollen ankle. That's when I saw him: the Sheriff. Daddy was talking to the Sheriff!

"What was with you last night? Hanging back like a hangdog," the Sheriff said, so low I could barely hear him. "Jimmy said you were a man of action."

"You've got to give me time," Daddy said. "I've got my family to consider."

Family. Daddy was talking about me?

"Hi, there, Sheriff," I said, coming up to the truck and making my presence known. If they wanted to talk about me, they could, right here in the open.

The Sheriff tipped his hat. "Hello, there, yourself."

Daddy pulled me to him, resting his hands on my shoulders. A barrier standing between them.

"Didn't I tell you to keep your old man out of trouble, and here he is with his meter past time." He reached for his clipboard, ready to write Daddy a ticket. He leaned in with his peanut breath. "What do you think I should do about that?"

"Um . . ." I looked to Daddy, who calmly took a drag from his Lucky Strike. His eyes gave me no hints at how I should answer. I took a deep breath. Told myself we had the money. "I reckon if he broke the law, he gets a ticket."

"Well, well . . ." The Sheriff tossed his clipboard back in the patrol car. Then he winked at Daddy. "You sure got a law-abiding little girl, Otis. Not loyal, mind you, but a damn fine citizen."

I waited for Daddy to tell him I was loyal. Loyal as all get out, but Daddy just tipped his hat and told the Sheriff good-bye.

THIRTY-FIVE
Right Here

That wind must've blown rain clouds over Holcolm. Before I could say boo, it started storming something fierce. The wipers chugged across the windshield, and the rain sounded like BB pellets striking the truck roof, making it impossible to carry on a conversation. Not that Daddy was in a chatting mood. He sat, stone-faced, his knuckles turning white, from either the Sheriff's chuckling or the nasty weather.

Daddy took a roundabout way home. From the way the road curved and the black-eyed Susans I saw along the way, I knew we couldn't be too far from Biggs Repair. At the top of a steep hill, even with the rain sloshing, I saw the tip-top of the gray painted barn. Daddy didn't slow though. Not that he would've. Keeping our No Biggs promise had to be easy for him.

Eventually, Daddy pulled into the base of our drive. "Give your mama her gift," he said.

The inside of the windshield had fogged over. The defroster wasn't working. Daddy cracked his window and wiped the inside of the windshield with his forearm.

"You're not coming in?"

"Can't." He leaned over and opened my door. Rain came down in heavy, slanting sheets. Our dirt road was becoming a muddy mess. "Tell her I'll be home after supper."

I didn't budge. "She's going to want to know where you're going." I surefire did.

"Need to go see Jimmy."

"But, Daddy—"

"This ain't the time to be difficult, Polly-gal." His voice was firm. "Now, go on. Show her your pretty dress. I won't be gone long."

I had no choice. He handed me a copy of the *Penny Saver* from the glove compartment. I put the newspaper over my head, stepped out into the rain, and did a run-hop as fast as I could on my hurt ankle to get to the front door. *Please please please keep your promise. No drinking.*

"Daddy will be back after supper," I called as I came in. Mama was in the kitchen peeling carrots and humming along with the radio. "He had to go see Uncle Jimmy."

"For what?" Mama asked.

"Not sure," I said, wondering how I got caught in the middle again. "Maybe a new shipment of televisions came in or something that he has to unload."

"All right." Her wrist worked that peeler double-time. "How'd the suit shopping go?"

"Good. Daddy picked a pinstripe suit. It's getting tailored," I said, from the hallway. I hid the bags from her. Daddy's gift was a surprise. He could give it to her himself. "Going to go study in my room."

"Your foot's not ailing you, is it?" she asked.

"Naw, just tired is all."

"Okay, baby." Mama finished the last carrot and switched to peeling potatoes.

I hung my new dress on the inside of my closet door, leaving it open so I could take in the sight of its folds. I'd tap the door closed if Mama came in. It being the first store-bought dress I owned in forever, I wanted it to be all mine for a spell.

I folded the store bag and stuck it behind my winter loafers. A pair of shoes caught my eye. Ones that weren't there when I left that morning. A pair of black patent leathers lay there, all spiffed up and shining, but they certainly weren't new.

"Tarnation." I couldn't get away from Timbre Ann's hand-me-downs. Now they'd just be on my feet instead of my back. Had Henri stopped by when Daddy and I were gone, or had Mama been holding on to the shoes for days?

I flopped on the bed. Forget studying. Forget Timbre Ann. Forget Daddy. Forget the Sheriff. I was sick to death of all of them. Sick to death of my life. Surefire, I might as well get lost in someone else's. I'd long since finished *Tom Sawyer*, so I got out *The Adventures of Huckleberry Finn*. Ask me, Huck was more fun than Tom anyway. I was glad he got his own book.

Fifty pages in, Mama knocked on my door.

"Supper's ready," she said, before turning back down the hallway.

I hobbled after her.

She'd done my nightly chore of setting the table. The bowls were dished out, full of steamy hot vegetable soup: potatoes, carrots, corn, and peas floating in bubbling hot tomato broth. The meal was perfect rainy-day-warm-your-belly fare. I took a slice of bread and spread a thick slab of butter on it, counting the chews in my head before swallowing. Even after my reading and my counting, my worries still had the better of me.

"Your daddy and I stayed up late last night talking, about you, about the baby," Mama said. "Being a big sister is a lot of responsibility."

"So is being an only child," I said, sipping my milk.

"Polly," Mama chastised. "Watch your tone."

"Sorry, ma'am." I wiped the milk mustache from my

lips. It wasn't Mama I was mad at. It was Daddy. Gone again. Maybe drinking. Nothing had changed. Nothing.

Outside the wind blew, rattling the windows.

Mama shifted in her seat. "Before your father gets home, I have something to tell you. I spoke to Henri a bit ago," she said. "She rang to tell me Timbre Ann saw you downtown."

What was Timbre Ann? A full-fledged spy?

"I thought she wanted to be a lawyer, not one of Hoover's FBI men," I said, all snippy. I took a bite of my bread and butter and spoke with my mouth half-full. "And we're not supposed to talk to the Biggses anymore. Daddy said so."

"Listen, little miss, your daddy and I together make the rules around here, not just him by himself." She drummed her fingers on the table, glanced at the clock on the stove, and then back to me. "In any case, I agree. It's better for Sam and Henri if we leave them be for the time being. I said as much to Henri. Said that with things heating up all over town, the letters, those fires, and all, it would be best to not be in touch outside of Judge Anderson's right now."

"Well, I'm not going there after school."

"Yes, you are. I don't want you home alone. Young girls can get into trouble by themselves."

"In trouble"? Did Mama think she had to watch me like a hawk, so I wouldn't end up pregnant like her? I barely knew any boys, let alone liked any! No one wanted to talk to me, not as long as I was friends with Timbre Ann.

"Then I'll go to the library. Get help with my long division."

"Why go there when Timbre Ann can help you?"

"I don't want her help," I said. My eyes grew steely, telling Mama she shouldn't want the Biggses' help either. We were to depend on Daddy only.

Mama grew silent. She blew on her soup, even though it was probably lukewarm by now. I felt bad. I knew she was missing Henri. Shoot, I was, too.

"What'd Henri say?" I asked. "When you told her?"

"She understood. She said she didn't like it any, but for the time being it was best." Mama closed her eyes for a moment while she rubbed her forehead. "Hate is nothing new. Not here in Holcolm. Henri said she could abide the nasty names, and me, I didn't care who shunned us as long as we had Henri, but setting these fires, whoever is doing such a thing is dangerous."

"Why now?" I asked. "Why are the fires happening now?"

"I wish I knew, Polly. All I can think of is some folks don't like change, and they will do anything to see that things stay the same." Mama's eyes were weary. "Someone is going to end up hurt, and it's not a matter of black or white. What's going on in this town is going to make its mark on everyone. Henri knows it, too."

"You sure Henri didn't come over?" My eyes flared at Mama, accusing. "Don't deny it. I saw those shoes."

"What exactly are you accusing me of?" Mama crossed her arms over her breasts. "I told you Henri and I spoke on the telephone. And, as for those shoes in your closet, Timbre Ann gave me those back at Pine Bluff. She slipped them into my handbag, knowing you'd need them for the funeral."

"Before she got new ones?" How desperate did Timbre Ann think I was? "She walked into a store barefoot?"

"No, not barefoot. I am sure she wore her socks." Mama sipped from her glass of milk, which was good for the baby. "But none of that has anything to do with being spotted with the Sheriff, which is what we were talking about."

I pushed away my soup. "Daddy's parking meter ran out. That's all," I said.

It was the perfect time to dump my worries on her. Tell her about how my gut flip-flopped with the Sheriff talking to Daddy. How he called Daddy hangdog. How he called me disloyal. But I couldn't. I just couldn't. Somehow Mama would think the worst of Daddy—not the Sheriff.

After dinner, Mama and I played three games of checkers before she said it was time to do the dishes. I washed. She dried. Thunder boomed so loud, neither of us heard Daddy come in. Just about when I'd given up all hope, suddenly he was there, dripping wet and scooping me up under the arms. He spun me around the kitchen.

"You're home," I said, breathing him in. I didn't smell liquor, or beer, not one drop. I smelled something else. Gasoline. He'd been to Teensy's. Just another poker night.

"Got back as fast as I could," Daddy said. "What did your mama think of your fancy dress?" he asked, setting me down.

"What dress?" Mama tossed the dish towel over her shoulder. She leaned against the sink.

"So you didn't give your mama a fashion show? Well, c'mon!" Daddy tugged me toward the hallway. My hands were still soapy. "Take a seat, Lisbeth," he called, "we've got a little surprise for you."

Daddy grabbed his suit bag. Mr. Matthews must've finished his tailoring.

We parted outside the bathroom. Daddy snagged a towel to dry his hair. "Go and change, but don't come out without me," he said.

"Sure thing," I answered.

I stopped, turned around, and hugged Daddy tight round his chest. He kissed the top of my head and swatted my behind.

"Hurry, we don't want to keep your mama waiting."

"Well, look at the two of you! So dapper and demure," Mama said, when Daddy and me appeared, all dressed up, in the open area between the kitchen and the living room. "Mother would be so pleased."

"We didn't do this for Meemaw, Mama. We did this for you," I said.

"Oh, who knows, maybe Irma wasn't such a battle-ax after all." Daddy winked at me.

Who was he kidding? He hated Meemaw as much as she hated him, but I guess he was trying to show some respect for the "dearly departed."

"Show your mama what else we got," he said.

I had been keeping one hand behind my back. The two scarves Daddy got for Mama dangled between my fingertips. I didn't want to scrunch them like the fancy blue handkerchief we were forced to buy.

"Surprise." I held them both out to her.

"Oh, Polly," she said, taking them and running the silk next to her cheek. "They're gorgeous."

"Daddy picked them out. He didn't even get any help from that Miss Caroline. She just rang them up."

"Is that so?" Mama asked.

"Yep, I got a thing for spotting beauty." He tugged Mama to him and kissed her square on the lips.

"Oh, Otis." Mama giggled, just like a schoolgirl.

"Ain't saying nothing that ain't true." He let go of Mama's hand to flip on the radio. He turned it from WKTO and found some bluegrass station playing a slow country waltz. "May I have this dance?" he said. I was sure he was asking Mama, but he bowed before me.

I got all shy. "I don't know how." I never had a real dance before. Just my piggyback dance in the woods.

"Daddy and I will show you," Mama said.

"Damn straight," he agreed.

Gruff words, but Mama smiled. She held out her right arm. Daddy took it. She bent her left arm and placed it on his shoulder.

"It's all in the counting. One-two-three, one-two-three," she said. Together, they spun as best they could around our tiny kitchen.

"Now, your turn," Mama said. I hesitated, biting a nail. "C'mon. Come dance between us. It'll be like riding a bike with training wheels. Don't be shy."

"What about my foot?"

"We'll be careful," Mama said.

It felt nice, dancing that way. Not at all like when they sat me between them in the truck, in the prickly quiet.

"Your debutante mama was born to be a dancer," Daddy said, as Mama stepped away to let Daddy and me go it alone. "She gave up parties and cotillions, all for us."

"Don't be silly," Mama said. "All I ever wanted is right here." She took in Daddy spinning me across the worn linoleum and patted her tummy. "Right here in this kitchen."

THIRTY-SIX
How in Hades

Grover Street Baptist was nothing like Trinity, the little church where Mama, Daddy, and I used to sing worship over worn hymnals. We hadn't been back to church since the bird poo incident. If Meemaw were still alive, I was sure she would deem us heathens.

Mama's childhood church had a mess of steps out front and a showy set of pillars that made the place look about as friendly as the Holcolm County Courthouse. The folks inside matched the cold-shoulder exterior. A buzz swept through the large hall, folks looking at us Baxters like we were possums on parade. Thank goodness, Daddy, Mama, and I were dressed to the nines.

Mama walked up the aisle first. There was Mr. Matthews, the store manager, who sold Daddy his fancy blue handkerchief. Seeing him up ahead, I stopped. I couldn't make myself do it, even in my pretty dress. My bandaged ankle made Timbre Ann's size seven shoe fit snug. If I had any foresight—a big lawyer word Timbre Ann liked to use—I would've had Daddy buy my own patent leathers when we were out shopping.

"Be brave. The biddies won't bite." Daddy looped his arm through mine. I did my best to hold my head high, proud to be a Baxter.

We stopped at the family pew.

"Good morning," Aunt Clara said, her teeth clenched and her jaw tight. She motioned for us to sit.

Mama stayed standing. She gazed at the open casket where Meemaw lay, ready for folks to pay their last respects. Her sandpaper cheeks were rosy with rouge. "Hard to believe Mother's gone. Really gone."

"That she is." Even today of all days, Aunt Clara couldn't be sisterly. She gave Mama a small tug and sat her in the pew.

Before I could give Aunt Clara a "leave her be" grimace, she turned to Eunice, the colored lady she'd hired to help with the twins, and said syrupy, sweet as a cherry cordial, "Eunice, be a dear and take the twins outside, would you now?"

"Yes, Mrs. Whitmire." Eunice gathered their things. Pacifier. Blanket. Diaper bag. Maybe it was finding out I was going to be a big sister, but today the twins didn't seem too terrible.

"Can I go, too?" I asked. "Eunice may need some help."

"Don't you dare," Aunt Clara, not Mama, answered. "My boys may disturb the service, but you are old enough to pay your respects."

I hung my head.

"Don't you talk to my daughter that way," Daddy said, his voice low. "I may be working for Jimmy, but we ain't yours to kick around anymore."

"I wouldn't be so sure about that," Aunt Clara said. She motioned to Eunice to go on and get.

"This isn't the time or the place," Mama said to them both.

"Think you can fill Irma's shoes, just because you inherited her house?" Daddy spat his words.

"That is none of your business," Aunt Clara said. Through the throngs of mourners, Aunt Clara waved her black linen hanky at Uncle Jimmy.

"It is too our business," Daddy said quickly, before Uncle Jimmy, fat as he was, could get to us. As the organ began to play, he whispered, "Hear we Baxters got more than a little something in that will, too."

That shut Aunt Clara up. Mama, too.

Ask me, we could have skipped the service. Our pew didn't register a word Meemaw's minister said. We all sat there wondering how in Hades Daddy got wind of what was in Meemaw's will.

THIRTY-SEVEN
Open Arms

Open Arms Memorial Cemetery reminded me of Brandywilde, the working plantation folks toured to see how folks lived before the War of Northern Aggression. The grass looked thick enough to curl up on and take a nap. The hedges all were clipped to the same height, as if the gardener had measured them with a ruler. But the grandest thing was the large-as-life angels laced into the metal gate that you had to drive through to enter. All pomp and circumstance. The perfect place for Meemaw to be laid to rest.

We wound around the cemetery, following Uncle Jimmy's LeSabre. Finally, the hearse came to a stop. By the time Daddy pulled over to park, Mama was half out of the truck and ready to go. She wrapped her arm around my shoulder and ushered me off, not waiting on Daddy.

"Y'all head on over without me," Daddy said. He dug out his tin of chewing tobacco and stuffed a wad under his lip, a sure sign he was pouting. "I know when I'm not wanted."

"What are you talking about?" Mama tapped her fingernails on the plastic clasp of her purse. A bee had been in her bonnet ever since the very mention of Meemaw's will.

"Can't a man console his wife?" Daddy asked.

"I don't know what you are talking about," she said again, all huffy.

Of course she knew. I surefire did. During the church service, when Daddy patted her knee, she jumped like she'd been given an electric shock.

I waited for Mama to smooth things over, a *Don't be silly, just don't think a church pew is the place to be lovey-dovey* should do the trick. Instead, she busied herself, checking her cried-out eyes in her compact mirror, when I bet what she really was doing was seeing if Aunt Clara was close enough to overhear her and Daddy having a spat.

Forget Mama. If she wouldn't take Daddy with us, I would. A funeral was a stick-together occasion.

"'Course you're wanted," I said. I grabbed his hand and then Mama's. A chain linking the two of them together—forever and always. "You gotta come. We're a family."

"Your father will do what he wants." She wrangled free of my grip. She snapped her compact shut. "He always does."

Mama stalked off, the kick pleat in the back of her skirt working overtime to accommodate her long-legged strides.

Daddy rubbed the balls of his palms into his eyes.

"She's mad I put Clara in her place back at the church. Well, it was her blasted husband that spilled the beans about the Battle-Ax's will."

"Uncle Jimmy? He told you?" I squinted at Daddy in the bright sunshine.

"Not exactly," Daddy said. "I overheard him talking about it to one of the fellas. I got the feeling it must be some big-time money from the way he was acting."

"What if he was lying? Stretching the truth," I said.

"Hell, why would he do that? Irma left him and Clara Pine Bluff. They're sitting way prettier than we are," Daddy said. He eyed the crowd of mourners. "Best catch up with your mama, Polly. I knew today would be hard on her. Swear on the Bible I didn't mean to make it worse."

"Come with me." I tugged on his arm. Did he have another flask? Would he drink while we were gone? "Mama needs you. She just isn't that good at showing it."

"Naw, mood she's in, I'm bound to make matters

worse." Daddy pointed to part of the iron fence. "I'll wait for y'all there. Promise."

I went to Mama. On my own.

Big bustling clouds rolled overhead. Not rain clouds, but fluffy ones that reminded me of the marshmallows Henri sprinkled on top of her candied yams. Meemaw had loved Henri's yams. So did Judge Anderson. He stood a few feet away from Mama, chatting with the mayor.

"Think Meemaw would be happy the sun is shining?" I asked, as I came up.

"I bet she'd be more pleased with the turnout than the weather. Mother liked being part of a big to-do," Mama said. "When Father was alive, she used to throw the best parties. Henri'd work overtime, cooking up a storm. Crab cakes, beef Wellington, cherry tarts. You name it."

My stomach rumbled. Mama's memories had given me a three-helpings hunger. Aunt Clara was hosting a luncheon later, and I sure hoped she didn't skip the normal funeral-day fixings—fried chicken and potato salad—in favor of hoity-toity watercress-and-cucumber finger sandwiches. Yuck.

"There you are," Aunt Clara said as we reached the

crowd gathered at the back of the shiny black hearse. "Why, I wonder what kind of a scene Otis will make when he finds out it wasn't Mother who left—"

"Can't we bury Mother before we discuss the will?" Mama sounded exasperated, but she spoke loud enough for the folks milling by to hear.

Aunt Clara rearranged her thin-lipped smirk into a solemn display—a performance for the passersby.

"Just as I was saying, Sister, money matters can wait," Aunt Clara said. "Look, James is ready to lead the procession."

As if on cue, Meemaw's casket was being taken from the back of the hearse. Mama and I fell in line behind Aunt Clara and Eunice, each with a baby on her hip. The procession snaked through the rows and rows of graves, making an uphill climb to where Meemaw would be buried.

"Who are those men?" I asked Mama. We were free to talk without Aunt Clara shushing us. My bandaged ankle had us falling a bit behind. "With Uncle Jimmy?"

"Pallbearers. It's their job to carry the deceased," Mama said, like that explained it.

"Shoot, I know what a pallbearer is," I said, exasperated.

The men wore white gloves, same as the ladies. I reckoned it kept their hands from slipping off the casket handles. They were brass and glinted in the sun. I felt sorry for them. Meemaw's big behind had to be heavier dead than alive.

"I thought just family got that honor," I added. Daddy may be good enough to do grunt work for Uncle Jimmy, but he still wasn't good enough for Aunt Clara. "Those men aren't cousins or uncles, are they?"

"No. They work at Pritchard and McLean, Father's accounting firm," Mama whispered back. "Hush now."

The preacher read from the Twenty-third Psalm. I should have been paying attention to walking through "the valley of the shadow of death." But standing so close to Granddaddy's grave, I felt more of a pang than when I saw his business sign swinging in the breeze from the bus. Though I'd been a baby when he died, I was filled with more love for him than I ever felt for Meemaw. A sin, for sure.

THIRTY-EIGHT
Surprise, Surprise

"Ashes to ashes, dust to dust." With that, the reading came to a close.

Aunt Clara stepped forward with a basket of long-stem white roses for us to leave on the casket.

"Go with God," she said, passing the roses to her right. By the time the basket reached Mama and me, who stood on Clara's left, only a few withered ones were left for us.

Mama elbowed me. "Go with God," I mumbled, tossing one.

"Go with God," Mama said.

At last the graveside service was over. Two colored men with shovels stood by, waiting for the mourners to leave. Folks circled around Aunt Clara and Uncle Jimmy, shaking hands and offering condolences. To my surprise, more than a few came over to Mama. I hung back as they shook her hand and said a few kind words. No one spoke to me. I tugged on Mama's arm. "C'mon," I said. I wanted to check on Daddy.

"Polly," Mama said, "one moment."

One moment was more like ten minutes. My insides were all fidgety. I'd had enough.

"Mama, I'm going to go find Daddy."

"Fine," Mama said, as Mrs. Riley, the town librarian, patted Mama's shoulder.

Mama was fooling herself. The caring and concern would disappear when night fell. Today she was a Pritchard, daughter of the deceased. Tomorrow, she'd be nothing but a black-sheep Baxter.

On the way back to the truck, my foot throbbed, stuffed as it was into Timbre Ann's old shoe. Without Mama's arm to lean on, I was lucky I didn't topple over.

"Hey, darling," Daddy called. I almost didn't see him, he'd wandered so far from the truck. He jogged over and ground his cigarette into the gravel when he saw me coming. "Where's your mama?" he asked.

"She'll be along," I said. "She's still graveside, lapping it all up."

"Well, reckon she deserves the attention. Her mother never gave her much," Daddy said. "Now, let's get you off that foot."

Daddy took me by the elbow and walked me around the truck. A hand-carved cane leaned against the passenger door. Daddy glanced over his shoulder, as if he was looking for a criminal, but his truck hadn't been broken into.

"Look at that. A gift," I guessed out loud.

"What? From where?" he asked.

Sam! I knew his woodwork when I saw it. But who had left it? I hadn't seen one of the Biggses at the service. Meemaw would have fainted if the hired help, other than Eunice, who was working, showed up at her funeral.

"Don't know." I fingered the fine cherry wood. It didn't curve like a regular cane, but instead went straight up like a walking stick. At the tip was a bird's nest, and inside were four eggs, the size and smoothness of riverbed stones. Lordy Lou, Sam had outdone himself!

"It sure will come in handy." I leaned on it. Sam had to have known my exact height. It fit me fine.

"Well, hang on to it. Someone spent a lot of time carving that." Daddy opened the truck door. He lifted me under the armpits and I slid on in.

I couldn't take my eyes off the cane. I admired the cuts, felt the smoothness of the wood, sanded and polished to a T. Daddy didn't notice all my fussing. He stood outside my door and lit another cigarette. He kicked at a few pebbles on the ground.

"Hope y'all are hungry," Mama said, walking to the truck. Daddy held the door for her. She saw the cane. Gently, I shook my head so she'd know I didn't give Sam away. She climbed in and started talking a mile a minute. "Clara said Henri's catering. Can you believe that? I can't. I mean, Clara dislikes Henri. Always has."

"So Clara hired a Biggs." Daddy shut Mama's door and walked around back to his side. "Wonder what Jimmy had to say about that?"

"Well, it surprised me that Henri agreed. Mother did fire her over those candlesticks, and Clara, well, Clara never liked her. Not since we were kids," Mama rambled. "Henri's not one to turn down a paycheck, not what with saving for Timbre Ann's schooling. I reckon even Sam would serve drinks if he'd been asked. "

"Uncle Jimmy'd never do that," I said, but a part of me wondered if he would. There was nothing Uncle Jimmy would like more than seeing uppity Sam wait on his houseguests.

Mama chattered on. "But that's Henri for you, willing to forgive and forget. 'The Heavenly Father holds no grudges,' I've heard her say, 'so why should I?' "

Daddy climbed behind the wheel. Getting in, his leg hit my cane.

It dawned on him. Mama's fast talking. My acting funny. All that Henri talk.

"This is about the Biggses, ain't it? Sam Biggs made that cane, didn't he?" he asked, his words slow and sure.

I had to tell him. I had to. "Uh-huh," I said.

"Damn." Daddy slammed the driver's-side door. "I should've known."

"There isn't anything to be upset about," Mama said. "Sam cares about Polly is all."

"He can keep his caring to himself." Daddy didn't turn his head but his eyes glared in the rearview mirror. "I can take care of my own."

"Daddy, don't be mad. He knows I like birds' nests. That I collect them."

"See? I'm sure he meant no harm," Mama said.

"I don't care what he meant. I'm getting tired of defending this family because of the Biggses." The steam that had Daddy boil over now settled to a simmer. He took a deep breath, spoke slowly, as if to a child. "Lisbeth, I know you've got your ways. Knew it when I married you, but I am tired—damn tired—of hearing it said it's a good thing Polly's so pale, otherwise I wouldn't know that she's mine."

"Who? Who said that?" Mama asked. She knitted her fingers together. *In. Out. In. Out.* "Who said such a thing?"

"Stoney Donner. For one."

"That's the man from the mill. The one you hit," Mama's voice quivered.

"Yeah, the one that got me fired."

"You were defending us?" Mama said. "Otis, you should have said something."

"Well, I'm saying something now." He reached over me and took Mama's hands, stopped her fiddling. He held her hands, wrapped his over hers. Then he opened them, like he was opening a book. "Look, Lisbeth. Look. You see that? You ain't colored. You're white. White."

He took my hand, too.

"So's our daughter. Ours. Not Sam Biggs's. He ain't her daddy. I am. You've got to let me be her daddy."

Mama lowered her head, the tears falling from her face. I patted her back, rubbing in circles, wishing we could stay in the truck cab, the three—no, there was the baby, too—just the four of us, forever.

THIRTY-NINE
Hired Help

The mold that had been creeping up the planks at Pine Bluff had been sprayed and scrubbed with bleach. The whitewash made the house look less forlorn. Inside, the place looked polished, elegant even. It must've looked like it did in the good old days, when Granddaddy and Meemaw threw fancy dinner parties. We were the last to arrive at the luncheon.

"Clara, you have outdone yourself," Mama said, as we entered the dining room. "Mother would approve."

"Of course she would," Aunt Clara said, all snooty.

Uncle Jimmy stuck a cigar in his mouth. He chewed the end off and spit it into his handkerchief. "This old house needed a lot of work inside and out. Good thing we got hired help for next to nothing. Coloreds will work for peanuts these days to keep their businesses from being burned."

Just at that moment, Henri, who had been in earshot,

placed a platter of chicken fried steak on the dining room table with a thud. Uncle Jimmy reached for it, but Henri slid the platter to the other side of the gravy boat, farther down the table.

"Eating now," she said, not one bit sugar, but all spice, "will ruin the taste of that cigar, Mr. Whitmire."

"In that case, girl, fix me a plate while I go smoke my Cuban." Uncle Jimmy strode away. The floorboards creaked under his heft.

I hated his talking like that. Hated it. Henri was not a girl. She was a grown woman.

"Here, Henri, let me help you with that." Mama reached for a plate and speared a slice of meat. She broke her promise. Here she was talking to a Biggs, and in front of everyone.

"What is wrong with you?" Aunt Clara took the plate from Mama's shaking hands and thrust it at Henri. "See yourself back to the kitchen. You're the cook. We have serving girls to do the serving."

Henri squared her shoulders but she did as she was told. She went back into the kitchen.

Daddy shook his head. He strode past us on his way out of the dining room.

"Otis," Mama said, but he kept walking toward the parlor.

What was it Mama had said? *Depending on who's watching, right can be wrong?* Daddy was watching; did that make Mama wrong?

Mama went to Henri. I followed Daddy.

In the parlor, colored men in red jackets and black bow ties circled around with trays. Some carried trays of those icky finger sandwiches. Others served the drinks. Lemonade or mint juleps, a pretty name, though I bet it had more than a jigger of foul-tasting whiskey. Which was just how Meemaw liked them.

I was flat on Daddy's heels until I neared the grand-father clock. A fat old man cut me off. I got around him in time to see Daddy, mad as all get out, stuff a tiny chicken salad sandwich into his mouth. Then, he downed a drink.

He didn't pick the lemonade, either.

I marched into the kitchen. No Mama. No Henri. It was a school day, but there was Timbre Ann. She sat on a stool with a schoolbook in her lap, not lifting a finger except to steal a pecan tart from a tray Henri had already fixed and that was waiting to be served.

"What are you doing here?" I asked. I hadn't seen her since she told me Mama was pregnant. The day I hid from her.

"So you're talking to me now?" she asked.

I didn't answer. I just stood there with my hands on my hips.

"Teacher in-service days, if it is any of your business," she said. "Aunt Henri made me come. She said it wasn't safe for me to be at home alone. Not with those fires."

Timbre Ann didn't offer any condolences. She just sat there, like she had back when Meemaw was alive and Henri was still working for her, her nose stuck in a book, as usual.

"C'mon, follow me," I said. I yanked her by the arm and led her out of the steamy kitchen, onto Meemaw's back porch, which was grand for a back porch, housing a sit-down swing and a ton of pretty flowers. Tarnation! Uncle Jimmy, the Sheriff, and some other men stood on the far side of the porch smoking cigars. I led Timbre Ann past them as fast as I could.

Were they standing around talking about the fires? I didn't stick around to find out but kept tugging Timbre Ann until we were farther away, hidden in the scrubby brush of the hedges that lined Pine Bluff, where we were safe.

"Why'd you drag me out here?" Timbre Ann smoothed her skirt. "To play hide-and-seek?"

I wasn't sure who or what I was mad at: Daddy drinking, Mama choosing Henri, or Timbre Ann not donning an apron, but that last crack of hers did it. I aimed all my anger at Timbre Ann.

"Henri's taking lip from Aunt Clara, and you don't lift a finger?" I spat.

Timbre Ann hugged the book she'd been reading to her chest. "I asked to work today. Aunt Henri wouldn't let me. She doesn't want me to have to wait on white folks. Pa, neither."

"So you sit on a stool in the kitchen, Miss High and Mighty. What about Henri—she can bow and scrape, all for your college fund?"

"Please. Like you care Aunt Henri has to bow and scrape." Timbre Ann looked me over as if I were a pesky fly she was batting away. "I've known you all your life, Polly," she said, sounding haughtier and haughtier. "You're not mad my aunt has to work. You're jealous. Jealous that even without a mama, my family does right by me. Makes sacrifices for me. That's it, isn't it?"

I balled my fists. I wasn't jealous. I wasn't!

"Peter told me so. Told me soon after he met you, but I didn't believe him. You're jealous," Timbre Ann said, singsongy. "Jealous of a colored girl."

"I am not," I said. I felt my cheeks get hot, like the

time I stomped on Sally Jean's foot. Timbre Ann had better watch it.

"Your mama's the town crier—and now, word is, your daddy's the town drunk."

I lunged at her. "Take that back. You don't know nothing about my daddy."

Timbre Ann spun out of my grasp and put the tree trunk between us.

"'Help me, Henri, there's no food in the cupboard.'" She rubbed her eyes, imitating Mama. "'Help me, Sam. I need a ride.'"

Anger lodged in my throat like a wad of chewing gum.

"We've been your cook, your chauffeur"—Timbre Ann kicked at the pine straw on the ground; a clump hit my hand-me-down patent leathers—"your shoe store for years. You Baxters haven't given us a thank you. Least today, we get a paycheck."

Before I knew it, I slapped her. But good.

Her hand sprang up to slap me back, but she caught herself. She stared at her palm like she was the one who did the slapping. "You aren't worth it, Polly. None of you Baxters are worth it." Her eyes narrowed, and she turned and ran. Right past the Sheriff and Uncle Jimmy. Right past Daddy.

"Look at that, putting that Biggs girl in her place," the Sheriff said. He hung by a clump of pines, the three of them having sauntered over from the back porch while we were fighting. "Didn't think you had it in you, Polly."

Big-bellied Uncle Jimmy laughed so hard, I thought he might cough up a lung.

Daddy didn't laugh. He sloshed his drink into the grass. A few drops splashed up from the ground and hit my legs and shoes. "C'mon, fellas," he said. "Show's over."

As they turned to go, my knees felt shaky. I slid my back down the tree and sat on the ground. I smelled it, then. Smelled it good. Syrupy sweet. Surefire, Daddy'd been drinking, but that brown stuff hadn't been whiskey. Daddy kept his promise. He'd been drinking sweet tea.

"Stupid! Stupid!" I threw a clump of pine straw as far as I could. My hand smarted. It stung.

No way, no how, could I take my slap back. And from the look I'd seen in Timbre Ann's eyes, she'd hold it against me until the day I died.

FORTY
Front Porch Chat

That night Mama found me on the front porch. I was staring into the dark, listening to the cricket chorus. Had I really slapped Timbre Ann? She'd said nasty things about Mama, about Daddy, about all us Baxters.

Still, two wrongs didn't make a right. Maybe she knew that. Was that why she didn't slap me back? Or was she afraid of what would happen if all those men saw her strike out at me, even though I'd started it?

"Awful late to be stargazing," Mama said, joining me. She had her sweater on over her thin cotton nightgown. With her bedtime curls framing her face, she looked like an angel. Too bad her daughter was the devil incarnate.

"What're you doing up so late? Something troubling you?" she asked.

Should I tell Mama about thinking Daddy took a drink? That after that slap, Uncle Jimmy made me a Shirley Temple with extra cherries? That the Sheriff tipped his hat to me when he left the luncheon?

"Nothing," I said. "Just couldn't sleep is all."

Mama raised her brow. My tone wasn't at all convincing, but she didn't push me.

"Mind if I sit with you? It's an awful pretty night."

I shrugged my shoulders. "It's a free country," I said, all lippy.

Mama paid me no never mind. She took a seat, sighed, and looked up at the sky. She'd only let me be for so long. I had to tell her something—sitting out here in the dark wasn't like me. Wasn't like me at all.

I *thump-thump-thumped* my heel against the half-rotted wood.

"What'd I tell you about that, Polly?" She laid her hand on my knee.

"Sorry." She put it there to get me to stop, but even so, her hand felt good. Warm.

"I know it's been hard lately," Mama said. "Change is hard."

"Yes, ma'am."

Mama breathed in the crisp night air. Shoot, I knew then that she'd let me be, that she wouldn't hound me any. Just knowing I had a choice in the matter made me want to spill my guts.

"Did you ever do something you wish you could erase?" I asked. Those cherries Uncle Jimmy plopped in my drink tasted sweet going down, but now they sat rock hard in my stomach. "Something you'd take back if you could?"

"Is this about you and Timbre Ann?" Mama asked. When I didn't answer, she fingered my bangs. They had gotten so long, they grazed my eyelashes. "Seems we always end up hurting the ones we love."

"Is that why you stole Daddy from Aunt Clara?" I hadn't meant to blurt it out, but there it was. "To hurt her?"

"Where did you get such a notion?"

"Daddy said as much. The night Meemaw kicked us out. You didn't deny it." A cloud passed overhead, blocking a good patch of stars and sky. "I was there, remember?"

"Well," Mama said, realizing I wasn't going to let it lie. "I didn't exactly steal him."

"But Aunt Clara was dating him first?"

Mama sighed. "You sure are grown, giving me the third degree." She pulled me to her. "Where to start?" she asked herself.

With my head against her chest, I could hear her heart beating. I hadn't forgotten that it was beating for two.

"In high school, your daddy was a star pitcher. Scouts came to look at him to play in the minor leagues."

"I know that part," I said.

"Well, he was good. Darn good. He could've made it

to the majors, but he hurt his shoulder hauling seed."
Mama shook her head, remembering. "When his big shot
got blown, instead of making the girls scatter, it made them
want him all the more. Clara was just one of many."

I chewed on a nail. "I can't imagine them liking each
other. Not now, not ever."

"Oh, your daddy was charming. Still is. And Clara
was quite the catch. Homecoming Princess. President of
the Future Homemakers of Holcolm. They were in the
same grade. Seniors. But they weren't an item; they'd only
gone out twice."

"So how'd you and Daddy get together?"

Mama smiled a faint, secret smile. "Well, on their
third date, or so, during her ironing, Henri'd gotten a rust
stain on Clara's best dress. Clara refused to come down,
saying she had not a thing to wear." Mama tilted her head
back, like she was at the picture show. I reckoned she
could see the scene playing out in her mind. "That same
day, I was off to a picnic at Clarke's Lake. Innocent
enough, Otis offered to give me a ride there."

"And you ate three plates of chicken?" I asked.

Mama cupped my chin. "You've heard this story before?"

"Kind of," I muttered, halfway mad that Daddy gave
me bits and pieces, that Timbre Ann gave me bits and
pieces, and that Mama hadn't a clue what I knew.

"Well, that's that. Your daddy took me to the picnic, stayed the whole afternoon, and we've been together ever since."

I knew better than to ask what came next. By the end of that year, she was pregnant with me.

Mama got to her feet.

One last question itched at me. "Mama, if Meemaw didn't leave us any money, who did? We did get something, didn't we?"

"Oh, sugar," Mama said. "That's even more complicated." Her eyes drifted toward a flash of light that flickered in the trees. Once. Twice.

I reckoned some deer hunters thought they'd get a jump on the season. Then they flickered again. Those beams weren't flashlights. They were headlights.

Sheriff Wilkes. What was he doing here? He drove by, taking a long gander at Mama in her thin cotton gown, huddled in her sweater, me at her feet. I counted to thirteen Mississippi, which felt like forever, before seeing the red of his taillights disappear.

"Bed now, ladies," Daddy said from the doorway. I had no idea how long he'd been standing there. No telling if or what he'd heard. "It's late."

FORTY-ONE
Deliver Us

My conscience got the better of me. It was a school day, so I set off early, before Mama and Daddy woke. I left them a note: "Going to see Miss Kilburn for math help." After my slap, no way, no how, would Timbre Ann wait at our willow. I had to get to her house before she left for school.

I took my bird's-nest walking stick. The swelling in my ankle was down, but I wasn't sure how it'd fare on the walk to the Tracks, but I was going to give it a try. I owed Sam a thank you, as much as I owed Timbre Ann an apology.

The entire walk, I watched the tops of the trees. They swayed. My only thought was, *Please please please let her listen.*

My ankle throbbed long before I neared their street, but as I turned their corner, it went numb. I could see their house, yellow with green shutters, sitting in the middle of the block, announcing: We may be colored, but we're proud.

As I climbed their porch steps, I noticed Timbre Ann's bike, kickstand up, Henri's straw welcome mat, and Sam's hand-whittled door knocker. I'd gotten it wrong. Everything about each of the Biggses—Sam, Henri, Timbre Ann—said the exact opposite: We're proud to be colored.

I reckoned it wasn't only long division that stumped me, but life stuff, too.

"Child, what are you doing here?" Henri said, when she answered the door. "Are you trying to get yourself killed? What if the Sheriff sees you?"

She ushered me inside. The hallway was cold. There was a morning nip in the air.

"He didn't see me. No one did. It's still awful early." I looked around the house. It felt empty. I hadn't seen Sam's car in the carport. Had he already left to take Timbre Ann to school?

"Thank heavens for that." Henri looked relieved. "Half the Tracks is up there, trying to put out that fire. It's bad. Been raging all night. I wanted to go, but Brother, he wanted me here by the phone."

Something close to panic rose inside my chest. Flames could leap out. Lick out. "Where? Where was the fire?"

"Peter—that boy that works for Sam—they got his family's store."

Henri didn't need to say the last name. I was out the front door—my walking stick under my armpit—and on the seat of Timbre Ann's bike, heading for Fulbright's, before Henri could call out after me, "Don't go, Polly. Most folks ain't going to want to see a white face."

Sure enough, they didn't. I dropped the bike a ways back from where the store once stood. Folks milled about with sweat rags tied over their noses to keep the dwindling plumes of smoke from getting into their lungs. I didn't make out one pair of eyes I knew, not Eunice, not Sam, not Timbre Ann. Lots of those eyes were angry. Why shouldn't they be? Someone white—like me—had done this.

Where was the fire department? It was made up of volunteers, but they should be here, doing something. Helping somehow.

I got closer to the rubble. I didn't recognize a thing. It was all gone. Gone. Just wood and cinder, no walls. No aisles stocked with canned goods. No money box where Peter could make change. No rice and beans. Not even any chickens hanging from the line out back. From the stench, though, I could tell that they had burned up, too.

"Thank heavens we were at my sister's. If we would have been here . . . ," a woman said, and sat on a salvaged kitchen chair, a blanket wrapped around her shoulders. She mumbled quietly to herself, staring at the smoldering pile of planks. That had to be Peter's mama.

"Have you seen the Biggses? Sam or Timbre Ann?" I asked. My eyes kept scanning the faces, but I still hadn't seen them. Maybe somebody was injured. Maybe they'd taken them to town.

Peter's mama didn't hear me, she just moved her lips. "As we forgive those who trespass against us . . . Our Father, who art in heaven." She was saying the Lord's Prayer over and over, as folks hugged one another, wiped soot off their faces, shed tears. She wasn't invisible to them, or to me, but no one knew what to do, what to say, which I reckoned was why she was praying. She had no words. The words found her. They found me, too.

"Thy kingdom come, thy will be done," I said, joining her.

My shy voice blended with her cracked and broken whisper.

"On earth as it is in heaven," several more voices chimed in. Together, we spoke louder, sounded less wounded, more defiant. "Give us this day, our daily bread."

Sam came and stood by my side. He took my hand. I leaned into him. Strong, solid Sam.

Not far from us, I spotted Timbre Ann. She'd been with Peter, hunched over, using broken tree limbs to poke through the debris. The ground couldn't be dry, not from the soaking rain a few nights before. Her feet had to be getting muddy. She was more in the woods than near where the store once stood.

"I'm sorry," I mouthed. Her jaw, right where I slapped her, was hard set. She didn't mouth anything back. Not an "I hate you." Not an "I forgive you." Still, I wished she'd come stand beside me, take my hand like she did when we'd skip down to the creek in back of Pine Bluff, but she didn't move. She stood using that tree limb like I used Sam's walking stick. It propped her up.

After another full round of reciting, I could hear Timbre Ann's teakettle voice join in with the murmuring music we were making, breathing and being the Lord's Prayer.

"But deliver us from evil," we all said together. The words echoed in my chest. Maybe she would, maybe she could, forgive me.

"Deliver us from this fiery evil," Sam said, sounding like a preacher. "It can't keep us down. Not unless we let it." He stepped forward, hugged Mrs. Fulbright. Hugged Mr. Fulbright, patting him on the back. "For thine is the Kingdom, the power and the glory, forever and ever."

No Amen came. Timbre Ann broke through the crowd, pushed shoulders and arms so she could get to Sam.

"Pa, look. Peter found this way over there. Behind those trees." Timbre Ann handed him a bottle. A beer bottle.

"A Molotov cocktail," he said, inspecting it.

I knew what that was. A bottle filled with gasoline and cloth that was then set on fire and hurled fast as all get out—before it exploded into shards of glass, gas, and flames. A firebomb.

"Stupid crackers got so drunk they forgot to light one," said a voice from behind us. A couple of folks chuckled, but I didn't see anything funny.

That unlit bottle still had something sticking out of it. A handkerchief. A blue handkerchief that was soaked through with gasoline.

FORTY-TWO
Truth Time

Sam walked me to the edge of the trees. He handed me my walking stick. "Timbre Ann's bike got you here; it should get you back to Chessup."

"Yessir," I said. A few folks looked back at me. Me, calling a colored man *sir*. Peter was one of them. He was still angry as all get out and I'd overheard him tell a fella, "Next cracker that bothers us is going to be a dead cracker."

With one hand, I gripped the handlebars of the bike I'd borrowed, not stolen—despite Timbre Ann's raised eye-brows—and got on. I hugged Sam to me. I could smell the wet miserable night, smell the smoke covering him.

"Sam, tell Timbre Ann I'm sorry," I said.

All the sadness that I'd been holding on to, feeling the cold eyes warm to me when they should have hated me all the more, came spilling out. Tears ran down my cheeks, but I wouldn't let them stop me from saying what I had to say. Sam needed to know.

231

"I slapped her. Back at Meemaw's, she said I was jealous. Jealous of a colored girl and I slapped her."

I sucked in my breath. I'd gotten it out. It didn't matter that Sam would hate me now, too.

"I know, Polly," Sam said. "She told me."

"You knew? But you've been so good to me," I said, all confused. "You made me that walking stick, a thing of pure beauty, and how do I show my thanks, I go round slapping your daughter."

"They don't have a thing to do with each other. I made you that walking stick because Timbre Ann said she saw you hobbling. I saw a need and I offered what I could to fill that need," Sam said. He opened his arms wide, gestured to the folks milling about. "You see a need, and you fill it. Black or white, don't matter. A need is a need. Henri taught me that."

"'A need is a need,'" I repeated.

Sam squinted in the sun that was now poking through the plumes of smoke. "Isn't that why you started that prayer?"

I did that as much to fill my own need as Peter's mother's. Something, anything had to be done to ease the pain—hers and mine.

I tried to say as much, but Sam stopped me. He tapped my chest. "You listened to your heart. You listen with that the next time you think about raising your hand." Sam smudged his fingers over the last of my tears. "Striking out is never the answer. Look what happened here."

I didn't have to look. What I saw, what I smelled, would stay with me forever.

He gave me one last squeeze. "Now, get home safe. I have a feeling you and your mama are in just as much danger as the rest of us."

"Yessir."

Mama and I *were* in danger, but not the kind Sam suspected. Once I was out on the road, pedaling home alone, I said it out loud, what I'd been denying since I saw it. That blue handkerchief. "Daddy. He's in on those fires."

I rode home. I couldn't hide out the entire school day, even if I wanted to. I had to check. Check Daddy's drawer for that handkerchief. I hid Timbre Ann's bike in the woods back behind our house, where Daddy wouldn't spot it.

Mama was in the kitchen. She had her feet propped up on Daddy's chair. Her fingers moved in and out, in and out, but not out of worry. She was crocheting a baby blanket.

"Polly, what're you doing here?" She hopped up. "Did school get out early?"

Should I tell her? No. I needed to be sure. That store had to sell more than one of those fancy kerchiefs. Maybe it wasn't Daddy's. I had been wrong about so many things already. So many. Maybe I was wrong about this, too.

"I was too upset about Meemaw. Miss Kilburn sent me home," I lied, running my fingers over the tip of my walking stick.

"Oh, goodness. We should have let you stay home today." Mama kissed my forehead.

Was she giving me the business? I was sure Henri had called her the minute I hopped on Timbre Ann's bike, but it was Mama that leaned on Henri, not the other way around.

"I'm going to go lay down." I headed for my room, hoping she couldn't smell those dead chickens, but Mama made me stay.

"I know you're tired, honey, and this is bad timing, so soon after Meemaw's death, but we need to have a talk." Mama sounded serious. She took a seat at the kitchen table and cleared the balls of yarn. "C'mon, sit down."

I took the seat she was offering. What did she want to talk about? Was I wrong—had Henri called her?

"Last night you asked me about that will money. About where it came from, if it wasn't Mother that left it to us."

"Yes, ma'am," I said. Last night felt like forever ago.

Mama went to the counter, where an open box of donuts sat. She got out two plates and brought one back for each of us. "Well, that money came from my father. Your granddaddy."

"What?" I saw his name as it was on the grave marker: Alabaster Alexander Pritchard. "But Granddaddy died forever ago."

"See, that's the complicated part." Mama grimaced, but kept on as if she had rehearsed what she was going to say. "Before you were born, he set up something called a trust. Mother controlled the interest, making me beg for a penny at a time, but now, what with her passing, I control the interest myself."

Mama had been hiding money from us. Just like Daddy thought.

"That's how you paid the Sheriff, isn't it?"

"Yes." Mama got up, poured me a glass of milk to go with my donut. "It's okay to be mad. I deserve it. Your daddy was a bit mad, too."

"You told him?"

"Yes, sugar, I did." She handed me the milk. I didn't want it. "I haven't been giving your daddy a fair chance, so I decided to come clean—with him, and with you."

I was so tired from breathing that smoke, seeing all

those sad faces. Whatever it was Mama wanted to confess, I wasn't sure I had the heart to hear it, but she went on.

"To get even a dime, Mother made me promise not to say anything. So I didn't." Mama added a bit of the milk she had poured for me into her coffee. She stirred it. "Oh, and we had to go to Sunday dinners."

So that's why those Sunday dinners were more punishment than family pleasantry. Poor Mama. She'd always been at Meemaw's mercy. Too bad her father couldn't have willed her Meemaw's love.

"Mother's tight fist was good for one thing. That interest has been mounting and mounting," Mama said. "It might even be enough to give this family a second chance. To buy Teensy's—like your daddy's been wanting to do."

Daddy must have told her everything—well, almost everything. I had no clue that Mama had known Daddy was so serious about buying Teensy's.

"But both of us, sweetie, wanted to talk it over with you."

"Why?" I stared at my donut. My stomach hadn't settled, not after all I'd seen. I wasn't the least bit hungry.

"Well, that trust, it isn't truly my money, or your daddy's. We can use the interest since I oversee it, but the principal part of the trust, Polly . . . that money is yours."

"What?" I said, reeling. How could it be mine?

"Your granddaddy, he left it to you."

FORTY-THREE
Not One

Mine? Mama had to be razzing me. If she wasn't, somewhere there was a stack of bills thicker than the ones Sam had been saving for Timbre Ann. How? Why? How was it fair that we should get a ton of money when Peter's family now had nothing?

"We can talk about it later with your daddy, but I wanted you to know. Wanted you to think about it," Mama said.

She held out her hand and led me into the living room. We stopped at the bookshelf and she got down one of the two pictures of Granddaddy that we had. There was a sil-ver-framed photo of him in a top hat and three-piece suit. I always thought that wearing it, he looked like a magician. With his counting trick, and now by making money appear out of thin air, maybe he was one.

"This was taken at the wedding," she said. "My wed-ding. Even though I was pregnant—with you—he insisted we all dress up." She used the cuff of her sweater and dusted her father's photo. "My guess is, he also did it to get your grandmother's goat."

Mama meant it to be funny, but I didn't laugh. I reckoned she didn't like being used to get under Meemaw's skin any more than I liked being caught in the middle between her and Daddy.

"Bet him leaving me that trust drove Meemaw batty. Is that why he did it?"

Mama took my hand. "Don't you even think such a thing. Your granddaddy thought you hung the moon. Always counting your fingers and toes, announcing, 'Lisbeth, she's perfect. Perfect.' He would've wanted every penny to go to providing for you. That's why I thought it best we buy Teensy's."

"It wasn't Daddy's idea?" He hadn't twisted Mama's arm?

"No." Mama sat on the arm of the sofa. "He thought it was a good one, though. Said buying Teensy's is a way to keep providing for us"—she patted her tummy—"for years to come. Me, I just don't want him working for Jimmy."

I felt trapped. For once, Mama was on Daddy's side, and here I was, on the other. I had to know for sure if that handkerchief was his.

"Got to practice my vocabulary," I said, getting up off the arm of the sofa. "Class spelling bee is coming up."

She handed me Granddaddy's photo to take back to my room. "Then you best get to it."

I headed down the hall, then ducked into the bathroom. I counted to twenty-one Mississippi before checking on Mama. She sat at the kitchen table and was back knitting the baby blanket.

I crept into their bedroom. I tugged on the sock drawer, moved all the rolled-up socks around, and found a stack of hankies, way in the back. One. Two. Three. Four. Five. Six. All half threadbare from overuse. Not one was fancy. And not one was blue.

FORTY-FOUR
What Little I Loved

I knew that handkerchief wouldn't be in Daddy's drawer. I'd seen it with my very own eyes, sticking out of that beer bottle like a candlewick, ready to be lit with a match and to flash, lightning quick, causing a full-fledged fire. Still, I had hoped that what I thought was the gospel truth really wasn't. That those headlights the Sheriff flickered hadn't been a sign. That somehow Daddy hadn't snuck out and then gotten back in the house without Mama or me knowing.

I hadn't heard a sound last night. Not a sound. No dogs barking. No crickets chirping. I didn't hear Daddy's truck rumbling away, but the Sheriff had to have seen Mama and me on the front porch. He had to have known Daddy couldn't just drive over to the Fulbrights' without getting caught. Why, I bet he swung back for Daddy, picked him up, and they'd gone off together in that patrol car, not to police the law, but to break it.

Hands shaking, I closed Daddy's drawer and picked up Granddaddy's photo from where I laid it on their bed. Like the spy that I was, I crept back to my room.

I didn't understand why some folks just got one side of the penny-heads-over and over. Not me. I'd get a heads, followed by a tails. Always and forever.

Why couldn't today just have been the morning Mama told me good news? That Granddaddy loved me so much, he made sure I was provided for, just the way Sam had pinched pennies for Timbre Ann. But no. Tails had to come up, and it made things worse than ever.

My gut screamed, *How could you? How could you be in on those fires?* even though my voice couldn't. Mama would hear me. Instead, I yanked open my dresser drawer. There were my nests, all three of them. The one I'd taken on Timbre Ann's birthday, and the other two I found in the woods. I grabbed the one nearest me and hurled it against the wall.

It shattered. Bits of mud and pine straw and dry grass sprang back, raining on my bed.

I grabbed another. Daddy's denim shirt that lined the drawer came with it and dangled from a twig. I balled the shirt in my fist, hurling it instead. The buttons smacked the wall, stopping me from doing any more damage.

I put the nest back next to the one I'd taken from Timbre Ann's yard. I shut the drawer, knowing I'd be no better than Daddy if I threw the last two, if I ruined what little I loved.

FORTY-FIVE
Prayed Once

I sat in my room for what felt like hours. I couldn't go to the police station. The Sheriff was in on those fires for sure. I couldn't call Sam. He didn't have Daddy's temper, but I didn't want Timbre Ann to know she was right, that her father was better than mine. Always was. Always would be. No. No. I had to talk to Daddy myself. I just had to find the right time.

He was gone all afternoon, but he made it home for supper.

"Look what I've got!" he said, as he came in the back door. He pounded his boots on the last step. "Polly's favorite dessert. Cherry pie."

"My favorite is pineapple upside-down cake," I said. I loved it almost as much as Henri's coconut cake. If Henri and Timbre Ann knew that, Daddy should, too.

"Shucks," he said, handing the pie to Mama. He smooched the top of my head. "You can't blame a guy for trying, can you?"

I bit my lip. Silence. Dead silence.

"No, sir," I said. Not because I'd wanted to, but because I had to. Mama was giving me a "watch your mouth" look while she dished the supper plates.

"Sounds like your mama got a chance to tell you the big news." He took three glasses from the cabinet, filled each with milk. "In a few weeks' time, Teensy's will be mine. Imagine me, a business owner."

"Sure is something," I said. He'd never get some flier wrapped around a brick tossed through his window.

He tried to grab all three glasses but he couldn't do it. "Need your help, Polly-gal."

I snagged two of the glasses. Daddy took a plate and the one remaining glass.

"Aren't we quite the team?" Mama said. "All working together."

"Damn straight," Daddy said.

Soon as we sat down, I reached for the silverware glass in the center of the table. I got out a knife and fork and then passed the glass to Mama, rather than to Daddy.

I shoveled in some spinach and worked at cutting my thick pork chops into bite-sized cubes. I reckoned if my mouth was full, I wouldn't have to talk much.

"Hungry, are you?" Daddy asked.

"Uh-huh," I said, between chews.

"Polly, manners," Mama said. Meemaw may be dead,

but her commandments were written in stone. No eating before praying.

"Yes, ma'am." I put my fork down, clasped my hands together, and was all set to say the rub-a-dub-dub prayer when Daddy broke in.

"Let me." He rested his arms on the table, palms up. Mama took one hand, I took the other. Each of us bowed our heads.

"I thank you for this food," Daddy started. No "Dear God." No "Almighty Lord." No "Our Father." "I thank you for our growing family." Mama looked up, winked at Daddy. He smiled. Both kept their heads only partially bowed. Me—I stared at my spinach. I prayed once today, with Sam, with Timbre Ann, with all the folks at the Fulbright fire, and my heart had been praying ever since. *Please please please let me be wrong*—but I wasn't. I had gone looking for Daddy's blue handkerchief, when I knew right where it was: stuffed in that beer bottle.

"I thank you for my new business. Our new business: Baxters' Gas-n-Sip."

My stomach churned. I smelled those dead chickens. Saw that blue handkerchief. Heard the sound of all those voices praying.

"Amen," Mama said.

I pushed away from the table and toppled my chair. The vomit rose as I ran.

FORTY-SIX
Ginger Ale

Mama followed me to the bathroom. She held my hair while I upchucked. My lunch, leftovers from Meemaw's funeral luncheon, filled the toilet. I couldn't stop. Even when my belly was empty, I kept gagging. Dry heaves. It wasn't the food I needed to get out, but the truth.

But what good would it be to tell Daddy what I knew? He could still drive off while Mama and I were asleep and use his great pitching arm to throw those Molotov cocktails. Shoot, soon as the ink was dry on the purchase papers, I bet he'd even use gas from his pumps at Baxters' Gas-n-Sip.

No, talking would do no good. I had to think of something else. Something to stop him.

Mama felt my forehead. "You don't have a fever. That's good."

After I rinsed my mouth with that icky mouthwash, she walked me to my room.

"Here, let me help you get your pajamas on."

"I'm too sick to bother changing."

"Oh, all right." She tucked me in. My covers felt good. Warm.

"Sorry your stomach is upset, darling. Especially tonight, when we were celebrating." Mama went to the window, pulled my checkerboard curtains closed.

I heard a noise. Were those Daddy's boots on the back stairs? It was dark, but it was too early for him and the Sheriff, and whoever else from the Klan and the Council went with them, to terrorize the Tracks. Folks were still eating supper.

Heavens. The truck engine turned over.

I threw back my covers. "Where's Daddy going?"

"To go get you ginger ale. It'll help settle your stomach." Mama helped me lay back down. "Get some sleep. That and the ginger ale should have you feeling better."

I nodded off, but I woke when Daddy got back with the ginger ale. He brought me Saltines, too. The same kind Mama ate when she was so sick—morning sick.

My bed didn't have a headboard, so I sat up and scooted so I could lean my back against the wall. I fingered a piece of dry mud—mud that had been a part of the bird's nest that I'd hurled—and ate a handful of those crackers. They stuck in my throat.

I slowly drank the ginger ale.

"Daddy, where's that blue handkerchief?"

His brow furrowed. "In the laundry, Polly-gal. Where else?"

"Oh," I said. He rattled off his answer too quick. He was lying. Did he know I was, too? That I'd seen it sticking out of that bottle?

"How's your stomach?" He sat on the edge of my bed. "Better?"

"Yeah, a bit."

"Good to hear. You had your mama and me mighty worried. I've never seen you like that." He looked like he wanted to brush my bangs from my eyes, like Mama always did. Instead, he scratched his forearm. "Is something bothering you? That trust fund? 'Cause your mama didn't tell us? Or do you not want me to buy Teensy's?"

"No, no. Just sick is all." I stared at the top of his head, where his ball cap would be if we were outside. That way it would look like I was meeting his eyes, even if I wasn't. "Must've been the mayonnaise. I had some of that chicken salad leftover from the funeral. Maybe it went bad."

"Well, I'll toss it out." He got up to go. "I'll make flapjacks in the morning if your appetite is back."

He ruffled my hair, and I rolled over.

"Love you, Polly-gal," he said to my back.

FORTY-SEVEN
Sheriff's Sign

Around midnight, I climbed out of bed and slid on my sneakers, glad my ankle felt a bit better. I opened the window. It creaked. I waited, counting to ten, but neither Mama nor Daddy came running, so I popped out the screen and slung my leg over the windowsill. The garbage cans were there, up against the house, and I hoped it'd sound like the rumble of thunder if I hit one. It was dark, a starless sky, but we could get thunder for no good reason, even on the best of nights.

I scraped my shin going over, but I made it. Good thing our tiny pillbox house was a ranch and not a two-story. My ankle felt stronger, but it couldn't have taken a daredevil move.

The truck was in the drive. As quiet as I could, I let down the tailgate. There was an old tarp heaped in one of the corners. I curled into a ball and covered myself with it.

No telling what time the Sheriff would show. Or even if it would be tonight. But if it was, I aimed on being ready.

I waited until near sunrise for the Sheriff's sign, two flicks of his headlights. They didn't come.

FORTY-EIGHT
Spelling Bee

Lying out in the truck all night, I hadn't slept a wink. Figures, today of all days would be the spelling bee, drawn from our vocabulary words. Before lunchtime I crammed in as much as I could. I went over the words from the last few weeks, but I couldn't concentrate. I was eaten up inside about that blue handkerchief, about when the next fire would happen, about what I should do to stop it—stop Daddy.

Miss Kilburn had said the winner of the bee got to wear a crown. King or Queen Bee, depending on who came out on top. It was nowhere near being class valedictorian like Timbre Ann was when she left primary school behind, but it was my chance. If I won, I'd have a chance to show snot-nose Sally Jean that she had nothing on me.

The last hour of the day, Miss Kilburn lined us up—boy, girl. Sally Jean wasn't in my half of the contestants. Beverly was. Tom Ricketts got stuck between us. It didn't

matter if a boy or a girl won. It was every speller for him—
or herself.

"All right, class, this is our first bee of the school year.
We will have four more before summer vacation. At the
end of the year, whoever wins the most spelling bees gets
to keep this crown for the whole summer." Miss Kilburn
held it up. It wasn't made out of construction paper or plastic. I couldn't rightly tell what it was made out of—maybe
papier-maché. It was painted a shiny gold, and big ol' jew-
els covered the five spikes, one for each spelling bee won.
All eyeballs in the room were glued to it. Surefire, no one
could want it more than me. I planned to win it and take it
home over summer break. I'd wear it around the house
when the baby came. Queen Bee Baxter had a nice ring to
it.

"Today's winner gets to wear it for a week. Then we
put it right back up here." Miss Kilburn gestured to the top
of her book cabinet. She set the crown on her podium,
right beside her list of words.

"Our first word is *reference*."

That was an easy one. I spelled it in my head as Matt
Pulman spelled it out loud. "R-e-f-e-r-e-n-c-e." He moved
to the back of the line.

"*Shampoo*," said Miss Kilburn. "Our next word is
shampoo."

Sally Jean chewed on her lip. Ha! She didn't know it.

"A sentence, please?" she asked.

"Of course," said Miss Kilburn. " 'Sally Jean has such pretty hair, she could be in a shampoo commercial.' "

Sally Jean got so happy she almost curtsied. "Why, thank you, Miss Kilburn. Hmmm. Shampoo. S-h-a-m-p-o-o." She rattled it off lightning quick.

"Correct."

On the way to the end of her line, Sally Jean crossed her eyes at me. She knew how to spell that word all along; she just wanted Miss Kilburn to compliment her bouncy blonde curls. Ask me, they looked better with bird poo dripping from them.

Miss Kilburn kept calling out words. I always got them right, whether it was my turn or whether I was just spelling them in my head. Tom got his word wrong. Beverly moved up behind me. She kept stepping on the back of my patent leathers. "Sorry," she mumbled, but I knew she wasn't. Across the classroom, Sally Jean giggled.

"*Temperature*," Miss Kilburn said.

"T-e-m-p-e-r-a-" Sally Jean bit her lip. This time I knew she wasn't faking. She shifted her weight from foot to foot. "C-h-"

I pumped my fist. Surefire, she was out. O-u-t. Out.

"Can I start over?" Sally Jean asked, eyeing me.

"May I start over?" Miss Kilburn corrected.

"May I?"

"Yes," Miss Kilburn said, "you may."

"But that ain't fair. Isn't fair," I said, before Miss Kilburn could correct me. "She saw me. She knew she'd spelled it wrong."

"And what did she see you doing?" Miss Kilburn asked.

I knew if I said nothing she'd drop it. Give Sally Jean another word. If I told the gospel truth I'd get in trouble.

"Ma'am, I was pumping my fist in celebration. C-e-l-e-b-r-a-t-i-o-n because she spelled *temperature* t-e-m-p-e-r-a-t-u-r-e wrong. W-r-o-"

"That's enough." Miss Kilburn raised her voice.

The class erupted. Some kids clapped. Others called me a cheater. Including Sally Jean.

Miss Kilburn silenced the class, by giving us all one of her nail-on-the-chalkboard looks. We all got quiet. Sally Jean smiled a sickeningly sweet grin. She got me. I was in for it. "Now, both of you take your seats."

"What? Me?" Sally Jean curled her fingers into a fist. "But that ain't fair."

"Isn't fair," Miss Kilburn corrected. "And I believe it is. Polly was out of line, but so were you for leading me to believe you had a valid reason to start again."

Sally Jean opened her mouth. If she said one word more, I guessed Miss Kilburn would send her straight to the corner to write "I will hold my tongue and temper" fifty-five times, like I once had to do. I kept my lips zipped. I'd learned my lesson.

Sally Jean shut it. She huffed back to her seat. I slid in mine, with one word playing over and over in my mind. *Justice*. J-u-s-t-i-c-e.

FORTY-NINE
Natural

Still high from the spelling bee, I decided to give it one more try with Timbre Ann. If I hurried, I might be able to make it to Laurel Creek, the one road that led to and from Washington High.

I cut through the woods that butted up against the back of her school. With my semisore ankle I couldn't run. Even so, I pretended Timbre Ann was beside me, matching my strides, urging me to go faster, like she had just a few weeks ago, when we'd begun racing to the Andersons'. So much had happened since then. So much that I needed to set right.

I got there right before the bell rang. I stood off in the trees, clinging to one of the pines, watching and waiting.

She came out the side door. Peter was with her. A gang of other kids, too. Tarnation. I was hoping to find her alone. Since when was Timbre Ann so popular? She walked along with them, laughing. She never laughed like that when she was with me.

I didn't get the chance to step out and say hello like I wanted. Peter pointed me out. Timbre Ann squinted, hunting for me. I waved, trying not to look strange as all get out, sulking in the trees the way I was. She turned her back, saying something to her friends before she and Peter walked over to me.

"Hey," I said.

"Don't hey me, Polly. What are you doing here?"

She didn't hold Peter's hand, but I could tell they were a couple. They stood shoulder to shoulder.

"I wanted to talk to you," I said. I'd rather do it alone, but there was no way Peter was leaving her side. Maybe he was even there as protection. Protection from me.

"To tell you I'm sorry." I couldn't look her in the eye.

"For what? For slapping me?" Timbre Ann stood there, making me face what I had done.

I met her eye. "I'd take it back if I could," I said. "I never should've acted like that. I was angry. Hurt. But that's no excuse. I told Sam to tell you I was sorry. He did, didn't he?"

"He told me," she said. She winced as if her cheek still hurt where I'd slapped her. "But, I'm not like my pa. I'm not like Aunt Henri. I don't forgive and forget."

"But what about that walking stick?"

"What about it?"

"Well." I bit my nail. "Sam said you told him I'd hurt my ankle."

"I did." She squared her shoulders. "I told him I was glad you got hurt. That I didn't know how it happened, but I was glad."

Shoot, Timbre Ann didn't need to raise a hand to hurt me. Her words hurt plenty.

"I also told him I'd seen you with the Sheriff."

"You and your *daddy*," Peter said. I'd almost forgotten he was here.

"Since when are y'all so buddy-buddy with the law?" Timbre Ann asked.

I kicked my shoes, heel to toe, heel to toe—Timbre Ann's shoes.

"It's not like that. The Sheriff isn't my friend. He warned me about playing with you. But I didn't listen."

"Maybe you should've," said Peter. "It's not natural."

I wanted to kick him in the shin, talking that way. "What? Being friends isn't natural?" I asked. "Since when?"

"Don't look at him like that," Timbre Ann said. "He's not hateful. He's just stating the facts. It's plain as day. It's been a long time since we were friend-friends. Long before you slapped me."

I knew that. I knew it. Still, I didn't want to hear Timbre Ann say it.

"Why didn't you slap me back?" I asked. "I know you wanted to. I could see it in your eyes."

"If I did, I'd be dead. C'mon, you know it's true," Timbre Ann said. She stepped toward me, lowered her voice, maybe so Peter wouldn't hear. "We're not like Aunt Henri and Miss Lisbeth, and even if we were, folks would- n't let us be. Not now."

"We are so," I said, trying not to cry. Timbre Ann would hate it if I cried. "What about our flour fight? What about that night . . . that night . . ." I couldn't say it. Could- n't say, *Polly, be my sister. I'll be your sister.* We weren't just salt-and-pepper friends because Henri and Mama made us, were we? "That night in the chicken pox tent. You asked me—"

"I know what I asked you. I wanted nothing more than to be a big sister," Timbre Ann said, struggling not to let her tears that were gathering spill. "Now, *you* get to be one. Your mama is pregnant, and my mama . . . is dead. I never even knew her."

Shoot, the day I slapped her, Timbre Ann called me jealous. Had she always been a little bit jealous of me— because I had a mama and a daddy? But, she had Sam. She had Henri.

Timbre Ann used her palm, swiped at her nose. She wouldn't cry. She just wouldn't. "But, things are different

260

now. Our fight, those fires—" She glanced at Peter. "We couldn't be friends now even if we wanted to."

I scraped at the bark of the tree. Peeled it off like a scab. "But sisters make up. They fight, but they make up."

"Don't, Polly." She took my hand. Stopped me from hurting that tree. "I wish there was a way, but there's no making up for this." She sighed, taking in the sight of our day-and-night-colored hands. "It's how we were born." She sounded as old as Henri. Older, even.

I swallowed deep. I didn't want Timbre Ann to teach me anymore. Not about how or why we couldn't be friends.

She dropped my hand. She went to Peter and took his. The leaves crunched as they walked away, same as they'd crunched when I climbed out of my window last night. Tarnation! I had meant to warn her. Tell her what I knew, even if it got Daddy in trouble.

"Timbre Ann," I called, but what came out wasn't about those fires. "I won. I won the spelling bee. The first one of the year."

They'd gotten as far as the school yard. Peter kept walking, but Timbre Ann turned around. She didn't hoot, she didn't holler, but a soft smile crept across her face. Before she could help it, it grew as wide as it would have if Henri had set down a slice of her coconut cake before her. It was plenty enough praise for me.

FIFTY
Run!

That night, after I was sure Mama and Daddy were asleep, I changed back into my after-school clothes and donned a sweater. I stuck my balled-up pajamas in my pillowcase before popping out the screen and climbing out my window. It was cold, colder than the night before. I shivered as I dropped the tailgate and climbed inside. Timbre Ann's smile, her proud-of-me smile, would have to keep me warm.

I snuck under the tarp and made sure my sneakers weren't poking out. With who knows how much time I had on my hands, I prayed, the same as I had at the Fulbright fire. Only this time, I said the Lord's Prayer silently. The words moved around inside me, some heavy-"forgive us our trespasses"-and some light-"on earth as it is in heaven." They kept me from nodding off. No way, no how, could I sleep past the sun. If Mama came to wake me for school and I wasn't in my bed, I'd be in a whole heap of trouble.

On my eighty-ninth prayer, I saw it. A light cutting across the tarp. One flick. Two.

The Sheriff's sign.

I held my breath. It felt like forever before Daddy got in the truck. My heart jack-hammered something fierce. I didn't hear the engine turn over, but we were moving. Daddy must've popped the stick shift into neutral and rolled down the drive.

When the engine did kick on, I wanted to pop my head out to see where we were. But I didn't dare. I couldn't tell, either, if we were following the Sheriff, or if we were taking the lead.

I shivered again and pulled my sweater over my nose to keep warm. But it didn't work. My chill was coming from the inside, not the outside. Truth be told, I was scared as all get out. I wanted someone—anyone—to be there with me, to do what had to be done. To stop Daddy.

The truck climbed a hill and I slid. I grabbed onto whatever I could, a piece of coiled rope or something, and held on. My fingers were near to giving out when finally we stopped. The truck rumbled as Daddy cut the engine. My gut sank. We'd gotten to wherever it was we were going.

Car doors opened. Slammed. Feet stomped around. They weren't even being quiet.

"Who has the beers?" a gruff voice said.

"I've got them." The man grunted as he carried the case. The pine straw crunched as he set it down. One by one, I heard the bottle tops pop and the beer fizz as it was opened.

"Careful now," a voice said. "Don't want to go home smelling like a brewery. Clara will have my hide."

Even before he said his wife's name, I knew it was Uncle Jimmy. I couldn't rightly say I was surprised. He was a member of the Citizens Council. He hated colored folks. Always had. Always would.

"That's right, and don't drink the beers," said another familiar voice. It wasn't the Sheriff. Or Daddy. "Pour them out over here."

"Sure thing."

"Uh-huh."

"Yes, Judge."

Judge? Judge Anderson? He was one of them? I'd never even heard him say anything bad about coloreds. Then, I remembered how he'd made Mama feel when she asked for that raise, suggesting she take that money from Henri. He kept that hate in place, sitting in the courtroom and pounding his gavel.

Beer fizzed and sloshed. Hearing it made me want to pee. I should have gone before I snuck out of the house.

What kind of mess had I gotten myself into? I could just see all those men finding me curled in a ball, wetting myself.

"Otis, tonight's your night." Yep. That was the Sheriff. "It's your turn to throw the juice. Start us off with a bang."

"What about the Judge?" Daddy asked. "He's here special tonight. Just to take out Sam Biggs."

Sam. Heavens! We had to be on the big hill outside the repair shop. Daddy and I took this hill home the night of our shopping spree. Did he know then that he was going to come back here? Had he been scouting for a good throwing spot?

"No, Otis. You've got the arm. This one is all yours," said the Judge.

"Hold that funnel still," said the Sheriff. "I don't want to light myself on fire."

The men chuckled.

I couldn't gauge how far they were from the truck. It felt like they were so close they were breathing down my neck. I made myself look, sneaking a peak to see if I could climb out without anyone noticing me. It didn't sound like I had much time to slide down that hill and get to Sam.

I moved the tarp. The coast wasn't exactly clear. A man in a red-checked flannel jacket had his back to me. He was one of the ones I didn't know. From the look of him, he was fat. Not Uncle Jimmy fat, but I'd bet on being able to take him in a race if he heard my sneakers hit the pine straw when I climbed out.

I eased out from under the tarp and gripped the side of the truck bed and tossed one leg over, the same way I climbed out of my bedroom window. I hit the ground with a soft thud.

"What was that?" Judge Anderson asked.

"Shoot, Judge," the Flannel Man said. "Just a fox or some such thing. Maybe even a deer. Don't let it spook you."

Only one set of headlights was on. The shadows were dark, crisscrossing one another. I didn't move a muscle. I was frozen, crouched behind the truck tires.

"Fine," said the Judge. "I trust you hunters."

"Ha. That's us. Coon hunters," said the gruff-voiced one. "Season open all year."

"They're holding a meeting tonight. Did you see all those cars?" said the man in the flannel shirt.

The men moved to peer out into the trees. I wished I could see what they saw. Were Henri and Timbre Ann there? How many cars?

"We can't go torching the place when we know folks are inside," Daddy said.

"Folks? Who said anything about folks?" This was the Sheriff. "What we got down there is animals all. Not folks."

How could the Sheriff say that? *He* was the animal, not the Biggses.

"Count me out," Daddy said, firmly.

What? Daddy was bowing out?

"Shutting down businesses is one thing." He sucked on his words like chewing tobacco he was trying to drain the flavor from. "Killing is another."

The silence was thick. Daddy tried to walk away. Uncle Jimmy stopped him. Backed him up against the tree.

"Hell, it ain't as easy as that," he said. "You got a job to do. I paid you."

"I'll give it back. We got our own money now."

Uncle Jimmy laughed. His big belly rumbled. "You mean your wife's money. Your kid's money. You don't have a damn thing."

"I got a family," Daddy said. He stood chin to chin with Uncle Jimmy. "That's what I got."

"A deserter, huh?" the Sheriff said.

"Too bad."

"That's a shame," the other men grumbled.

Daddy snorted. "I'm leaving."

"Before you hightail it out of here, you should know an interesting piece of evidence—a blue handkerchief— was left at the Fulbright fire. Ain't that yours?"

"Why you son of a bitch, you took that handkerchief

from me at Irma's funeral. Used it to clean off your lapel. Said I splashed tea on you," Daddy said.

"Hell, I know that," said the Sheriff. He walked away, smug. "But a court of law won't. Will it, Judge?"

"No," said the Judge. He put on his courtroom voice. "You were there the night of the Fulbright fire, weren't you, Otis?"

Daddy shrugged his shoulders. Played it tough. "Yeah."

"And you threw a bottle, didn't you?"

Daddy didn't answer.

"Maybe not the one with the blue handkerchief. I hung on to that," said the Sheriff. "For safekeeping."

Daddy kicked at the dirt. I knew from his face, he was holding it all in. He wanted to kick the Sheriff.

"But you threw one, didn't you, Otis?" the Judge asked. "Tell the truth now. All these men saw you. You threw one, didn't you?"

No. Daddy, no.

"Yeah." Daddy struggled to keep his chin up. "Yes, dammit, I threw one."

"See, you ain't so innocent," the Sheriff said. "And if the feds come poking around our backyard, they're going to have your hanky to blow their rabble-rousing noses on."

The Judge grinned. "You're our insurance policy,

Otis. That's why Jimmy threw money at you. Down and out, you'd do anything for a dollar."

"What?" Daddy asked, looking like a deer in headlights.

"You are one dumb patsy," said Uncle Jimmy. "Even dumber than Clara said you'd be."

That's all it took. Daddy pounced. He pelted Uncle Jimmy with a blow to the stomach. Another to the chin. "I ain't no patsy," he kept saying over and over. Flannel Man pulled him off.

"A patsy who acted alone," said Judge Anderson.

"Alone, huh?" Daddy turned left, turned right. With nothing left to do, he ran for it. I was about to take off after him when Flannel Man wrestled him to the ground. They rolled one over the other, until Daddy was pinned. Fists flew. The other men circled round, shouting, "Yellow belly! Nigger lover!"

"I got him. I got him," the gruff-voiced one said. Locked his arms behind him. Pulled him to his feet.

The Sheriff sauntered over. Socked him in the gut. The face. The nose. I closed my eyes, and stopped counting the licks. I could still hear them though—the sound of skin hitting skin. When I opened my eyes, Daddy was bent over, choking. Blood and spittle hung from his mouth. The Sheriff wasn't about to let up.

Near the truck tire was a rock. I grabbed it. Hurled it. "Leave him be."

"Polly." Daddy coughed. Hunched over, hands on his knees, he struggled to stand up straight.

I stood for him.

Flannel Man made his move.

"Run, Polly-gal, run!" Daddy called, as the Sheriff's boot kicked him to the ground.

FIFTY-ONE
Biggs Repair

I did as Daddy said. I ran down the hill. Ran like the dickens. Flannel Man shot off, too. I could hear his raggedy breathing, his chest huffing and puffing behind me.

"Stupid kid," he yelled. "Get back here!"

I didn't check over my shoulder to see how close he was. I didn't care, so long as he stayed behind me. There was no telling how long it would take before they started throwing those Molotov cocktails. Daddy's words, *"—I got a family. That's what I've got—"* echoed in my ears. Daddy meant me. Mama. The baby. No matter what Timbre Ann said, my family included more than just us Baxters; it also included the Biggses. It always had.

"Sam! Henri! Timbre Ann!" I called. If they heard me, they didn't come out. I shouted again. Screaming and running was no good. I lost my footing and fell. I bit my lip. My ankle throbbed.

I stayed down and slid on my bottom, using my hands to push against the dirt. I was almost there. Almost there.

"Get out," I yelled. "Get out of there!"

I'd gotten to my feet and finally turned to check behind me. Flannel Man was gone. He wasn't following me. Still, I didn't slow. I dodged in and out of the parked cars; there had to be a dozen or so. There were too many people inside. Someone was going to get hurt. Daddy already had. He was still up there, bleeding on top of that hill, with the Sheriff and the others doing who knows what to him now that I'd run off.

I beat on the door. It was locked, as though Sam had locked up the shop for the night. Still, I knew they were in there. "Sam! Henri! Timbre Ann!" I called. I beat my fist again and again, making as much noise as I could.

Timbre Ann opened the door. Finally. "Polly, goodness. What is it?"

I grabbed her arm and tugged at her. "You gotta get out of here."

"Let go of her." It was Peter. He pried my fingers from Timbre Ann's arm. I didn't have time to argue. Not with Peter. Not now.

"Please, Timbre Ann, please. They know you're here. They planned it. Please."

I was crying. Near hysterical. Sam came to the door.

He took one look at me and said, "Everyone out. Go. Go home. We'll continue this another night."

Folks rumbled out of the folding chairs that had been set up around the garage. As they got their things together, I heard Henri: "Good night, now. Good night. Drive safe." She was helping to usher everyone out, but it wasn't fast enough. Over the scraping of chairs, the hurried good-byes, we all heard it. The sound of glass breaking.

With a hiss, Biggs Repair burst into flames.

FIFTY-TWO
Got Him

Folks screamed. Another bottle crashed through the window. It hit a gas can and in a flash, flames ate everything in sight. Sam's whittling. The sunflower drapes that Henri'd hung to give the place a little sunshine. Car parts. Another bottle exploded; folks ducked and shielded their heads and eyes.

"Lord help me!" "This way!" "Hurry!" "Heavens!" Folks shouted, screamed. Faces jumbled and mouths twisted. Arms and legs were everywhere, trying to get out. A moment ago, I'd been standing right by Sam, by Timbre Ann. They were gone. I closed my eyes. The smoke, the screams made them water. I couldn't see a thing.

"This way," said Sam. He was behind me. His voice was steady, so steady. Folks streamed by, coughing and wheezing, but I couldn't move. I stood there shaking. A beam, a crossbeam that helped hold the roof, splintered. I heard it crack, as if lightning had struck it.

"Everyone out!" Sam yelled. "Now!"

"Come here, child," Henri said. She scooped up a little girl who'd been separated from her mother.

Timbre Ann shoved me into the night. Folks darted through the cars, weeping and screaming. Some shielded their eyes from the flying embers and tilted their chins to the sky, as if they were watching a fireworks show.

Inside there were toaster ovens, radio parts, clocks, and cars. There was more gas and oil in those cars up on cinder blocks than in the one gas can that exploded and shot flames in every direction. Everyone was close, too close.

"Go, go!" Sam instructed. "Get as far away as you can! Climb up that hill!"

"No," I said, surprised at the sound of me talking back to Sam. "They're up there. That's where they threw the bottles from. It's not safe."

"You saw them," said Timbre Ann. "Who was it?"

Sam shook his head. "They're long gone by now. Go, go." Folks started moving, climbing the hill I just came down. Timbre Ann went. She did as she was told. Sam thrust me forward. "You, too, Polly," he said, as he headed back toward the repair shop.

What choice did I have? I started to go, to follow Sam's orders, when I saw him. Daddy. He was bent over, gripping his ribs, but running hard. He'd gotten away.

"Polly!" he yelled, coughing and spitting. "Polly-gal!"

He was searching—searching for me.

"Here, Daddy, I'm here!" I yelled. He couldn't hear me. My voice was swallowed and drowned out by the noise, by the fire and the screams of the folks who'd been at that meeting. Chaos. It was chaos.

A hand grabbed me. Squeezed my arm. "What's he doing here?"

Timbre Ann. She was back. Or maybe she'd never left—only pretended to do as Sam said. Peter was with her.

"He . . . he . . . was in on it. At Fulbright's." There, I'd said it. The gospel truth.

Peter whirled around. "What?"

"He did this, too?" Timbre Ann took it all in. Her family business burning. Folks she knew and loved were limping, screaming, crying. "This is his doing?"

"He tried to stop them. Tonight he tried."

"Yeah, right," Timbre Ann said. I didn't care if she didn't believe me. I'd seen Daddy, I saw the beating he took.

I scanned the trees, the faces nearby. "Where'd he go?"

"Peter?" Timbre Ann said. "I don't know."

I wasn't asking about Peter, but Daddy. I had to find Daddy.

I started running in circles. Heavens! Another boom

and a spray of sparks. I couldn't believe my eyes. The beam that had cracked earlier gave way. The roof, or a good bit of the roof, caved in. It came down so hard, it shook the ground beneath us.

"No!" came a scream. "Polly!"

I saw Daddy then: running into the repair shop. Climbing into the part of the building that was still standing. He had to be going into the fire to find me.

"Daddy, no!" I called, going after him. "Here. Here. I'm safe."

Sam caught me around the middle. He'd been crouched near the ground, helping an old man gather a blanket around his shoulders. All around us was the stink of burning flesh. It was worse than that chicken smell at the Fulbright's.

"Help me," Sam said. "Help me move him."

"But my daddy," I said. "He's looking for me."

Timbre Ann took my hands; she put them around one of the old man's feet. She took the other. I was moving, but in the wrong direction. Away from Daddy. He was in there. I had to get to him, as soon as we moved the old man. The three of us, we got him as far back as we could manage.

The man moaned as we set him on the ground. "Thank you," he said. He patted my hand. "Thank you."

I was about to tell him not to worry, that ambulances would be coming soon, but I didn't want to lie. I just looked him in the eye, to tell him how sorry I was. Sorry white folks hated. Sorry white folks set fires. Sorry he was in so much pain, with the skin on his arms gone, melted away like candle wax.

"Oh, child," he said to me. "This ain't your fault."

I waited for Timbre Ann to tell him it was. She didn't. Sam had wrapped her in his arms. He reached for me, was going to gather me into their hug, but I was already gone. I was running back toward the fire. I wanted my daddy, too.

"Polly, don't," Sam called after me. "It's going to blow." I ran—ran faster—as fast as my sore ankle would carry me.

Biggs Repair was broken. Those beams were its shoulders and now, now, its back was broken. Walls had caved in. Engine parts were melting. Sparks shot and flew.

I was running so hard I tripped. I got a face full of dirt, pine straw. I spit it out. I was on my hands, about to get up, when I spotted something shiny. If I hadn't fallen, I never would have seen it: Peter. He was off on his own, standing beneath an old pecan tree, taking aim with a rifle. A deer-hunting rifle.

"Next cracker that bothers with us is going to be a dead cracker," he had said.

"No, don't!" I cried.

Sam's hands were on me. Timbre Ann's, too.

I kicked, screamed, "No!"

"It's okay, Polly," Sam said. "Let us help you up."

They misunderstood. I'd been yelling at Peter. Not at them. I tried to wrestle away. That's when we heard it. A strange pop. Even over the crackle of the flames, the beams breaking, the shrieks and crying, we heard it. Peter. He'd fired that rifle.

Timbre Ann turned to Sam. "Pa, Peter—he had a gun."

We ran, all of us. Sam. Timbre Ann. Me. We only got but so far. A wall of heat slapped us back. Peter called to us: "I got him. I got him!" Proud, his rifle at his side. "One shot. I got the cracker with one shot."

"No, you didn't." It was Daddy. His face was so pained it was barely recognizable, raw wounds and soot. He bent to circle his arms around someone, man or woman, I couldn't tell. The body was at his feet. He tried lifting it but he couldn't. He couldn't do it on his own. I ran forward to help, to help him get out of there before the place blew. Timbre Ann and Sam did the same.

Sam got to Daddy first. He reached down to help him with the body he was struggling to carry—that body, dead or alive, that he wouldn't let go of.

"No, I've got her. Go," said Daddy. He tried to block the body, but he couldn't. Sam dropped to his knees. He wailed, his chest, his heart breaking.

Timbre Ann stopped cold. She knew it. I knew it. Knew who the body was that Daddy was carrying. Knew exactly who it was that made Sam cry like the earth had split open and swallowed him whole.

"Aunt Henri." Timbre Ann whispered her name. "Aunt Henri."

FIFTY-THREE

Step by Step

Timbre Ann, she went to Sam. She helped him to his feet. His legs gave out and he could barely walk, let alone run. Henri must've gone back in, to find another child or anyone else who needed help.

"C'mon now, let's go, she was the last one," said Daddy.

"How?" Sam asked. "How?"

"Her leg was hurt. I was helping her walk when she slipped. She's been shot," Daddy said. Flicks from the flames lit his eyes. He rubbed them, his eyelashes were singed. They must've burned with everything that had happened tonight. "We need to move her. The shop is going to blow."

I rushed forward, tears, soot, and smoke not stopping me one bit. Just like I had with that old man, I grabbed Henri's legs.

Peter dropped the rifle. In a second he was there beside me, helping me lift Henri. We lifted her as high as we could. "Lord, forgive me," he said over and over. "Forgive me, forgive me."

The heat made me scrunch my face. My arms ached. Daddy's had to hurt, too, but we kept moving. Sam and Timbre Ann, they walked as one. Their arms and legs moving together.

The terrifying sounds—the screams, the crackling— faded. All I heard was my own raggedy breathing. In. Out. In. Out. Like the way Mama fidgeted her fingers. *Oh, Mama. What would she do if Henri died?* I stumbled. We pitched forward.

"Steady now," said Daddy. "Careful not to drop her."

"Henri, Henri," I said. "It's okay. We've got you. It's okay." I muttered like a mama out to soothe her fussy child. Only thing, Henri didn't moan. She didn't whisper. Nothing.

Even with my nose clogged with smoke, I could smell the blood, heavy and sweet like syrup. I made myself look. The bullet had torn into her side. Up under her breast. Her flesh was shorn, like a trout I'd seen her gut for a fish fry. Her purple dress, her birthday dress, was soaked through. On her lapel, she wore a bluebird brooch. Timbre Ann had lied to me. She told me not to buy it so she could. How long had this night, this fight been building?

The blood seeped and spread. I couldn't look anymore. I focused instead on Henri's hands. She wore white gloves. Her church gloves. Tonight's meeting had been a special occasion.

"Here, lay her here," said Sam. We'd gotten as far as the old man. Gently, we laid Henri next to him. We barely got her settled before Daddy took off again. He ran. What was he doing? Looking for others? Others to move? To help?

I was about to take off after him when Henri gurgled with a wet-bubble popping kind of a sound.

"Put pressure on it," the old man said. Sam's suit coat was gone. He must've left it in the shop or else he'd already wrapped it around someone shoulder's. "Here, here, take this," the man said.

I grabbed the blanket from the old man's hands and held it to Henri's side, when I caught a glimpse of Daddy.

He'd run to the tree. The one where Peter hid.

He found the rifle, picked it up, and, with whatever strength he had left, he hurled it into the fire.

"What? Why? Why'd he do that?" Timbre Ann asked, as Sam grabbed the blanket from me. He held it tight to Henri's wound, trying to stop the bleeding.

"Making sure Peter doesn't end up like—" Sam's voice broke. He couldn't say it. He couldn't say, "like Henri," his sister, dead.

"Our Father," I prayed, wiping at my tears.

Daddy stood still, making sure his pitching arm had done the trick—that no one, especially not the Sheriff—would ever know Peter had shot at him, a white man. He threw that rifle to set things right—as right as they could be when everything, everything was wrong.

Done, Daddy turned his back on what was left of Biggs Repair. Step by step, he came back to me.

FIFTY-FOUR
Calling Me Forward

"You stay here," Daddy said, tugging open our front door. "I'll wake Lisbeth."

I nodded, numb. My eyes couldn't get used to the darkness, not after the orangey bright of the fire. I sat on the porch, dangling my legs between the rails. I kept my feet still. I couldn't bear the *thump-thump-thump* of my heels against the wood. The sounds of the night—crickets chirping, panicked screams, beams breaking, a single gunshot—all echoed in my ears.

Daddy went inside to face Mama. The cuts and soot on his face only told her part of the story, but he told it, all of it. I heard him, clear-voiced, tell about Jimmy paying him to get involved after the fire at the Castle fella's warehouse made the newspaper; about going along for the ride, but not throwing any cocktails the night of the Johnson's funeral home fire. About the Sheriff calling him a hangdog, and then coming to pick him up the night of the Fulbright fire. The blue handkerchief. And finally, tonight, his turning on the Judge, the Sheriff, on everyone involved. Jimmy and Clara setting Daddy up. And then he admitted the worst of it: he told Mama about Biggs Repair, and, finally, about Henri.

I cringed. Inside there was a shout. A scuffle. "Otis, no!" I sat still. I was done running to Daddy's defense. He deserved to feel her fists, her scrunched hands pounding his chest, not believing the words that came out of his mouth, that Henri was gone. That Peter killed her, but that he, Daddy, was just as much to blame. Drawers slammed. That's all I heard, until Mama's footsteps pounded the boards next to me. She'd tossed on a pair of pink pedal pushers and a lime green top, with the same sweater she'd had on over her nightgown the other night. The truck keys jingled in her hands.

"You coming?" is all she said to me.

"Of course. I got to take her bike back." Mama didn't ask me whose. I reckoned she knew I meant Timbre Ann's. I hauled the bike from where I'd stashed it, out in the clump of pines that grew so close together, so the bike wouldn't be seen from our kitchen window.

I climbed into the truck cab. After the Biggses', I didn't care where we went.

Nearly every light was ablaze. Folks spilled out from foyers onto their porches, speaking in hushed voices. I put the kickstand down and left Timbre Ann's bike right where I'd borrowed it from, in the back of the carport. The front porch gatherers didn't need to be so quiet; no one was sleeping, not for miles around—or in all of Holcolm County for all I knew. The fire would be talked about, chewed over, swallowed, and shared with the next neighbor down the line.

Mama stopped at the bottom of the stairs. "How is she?" she asked.

"Think you know the answer to that," a woman I didn't know said. Eunice, Aunt Clara's nanny, stood next to her. "Better question is, where is she?"

Mama gulped. Somehow she still believed Henri was alive. "All right, where is she?" Mama asked, leaning on the railing for support.

"Down at Johnson's funeral home, being cremated."

"What? Why?" Mama asked.

"So the Sheriff can't pin this whole thing on Peter," Eunice said. "Why else?"

Mama didn't hang her head. She didn't cry. She took in the news, letting it hit her the same as a slap.

The lady I didn't know turned to a woman on her left. "If the Sheriff finds out a Negro shot a Negro, he's likely to say we've been setting these fires ourselves. Then where will we be?" The circle of women *uh-huhed* their consent.

Mama climbed a few stairs. "Phyllis, where's Sam?" she asked. She knew the woman's name. Did she know everyone Henri knew?

"In the kitchen," Phyllis answered.

Mama went right in, making her way through all the people. I stayed where I was. Timbre Ann wouldn't want to see me. Mama may be innocent, but Daddy was guilty as sin, and I was a part of them both. I sat, hugging my knees to my chest, and it wasn't long before the folks who'd gathered on the porch went inside, leaving me alone—alone with the moon.

It was the same moon that hung outside our house— the same one I couldn't see, once that fire started—and it would stay there, shining until morning. It was the same moon Daddy had to be looking at, wondering if we were coming back home. I wasn't sure if this was a pit stop, or our final destination, and for once I left that decision up to Mama.

Behind me, the screen door creaked. From the size of the shadow spreading over me, I reckoned it was Sam. I was wrong. Peter sat next to me. "She won't talk to me. Can't say I blame her," he said.

My lips pulled tight, almost hurting from keeping in all the nasty things I wanted to say: "You tried to kill my daddy. It's your fault Henri's dead. Your fault everyone is crying. Your fault things will never be the same." A shiver ran up my spine. Peter had played his part, just as the Sheriff, the Judge, Flannel Man, and Daddy had done. And just as I had done, too.

"Soon as the sun rises, I'm going to go turn myself in," Peter said.

"Don't you dare!" I whirled on him. "Why do you think Henri's body is burning right now? Not to give the Klan and the Council satisfaction, but to save *you*. So you just sit there and live with it. Live with what you've done to Henri."

Peter buried his head in his hands and cried like a little boy. I left him there, knowing nothing would console him. Maybe nothing ever would.

Timbre Ann lay on the center of Henri's bed. She fingered Henri's once-white gloves that were a rust-colored brown from the dirt and the blood. A framed photo of Henri was arranged on the pillow next to her, a makeshift memorial. I hadn't known for sure that Timbre Ann was here. It was the first place I looked, but it was the only room in the house where the lights were off.

"I brought you a sandwich, ham and cheese," I whispered.

She made no sign that she'd heard me. The wind blew through the open window and the curtain shifted in the breeze, making the room chilly. A pair of headlights cut across the yard; more and more folks were arriving, paying their middle-of-the-night condolence calls.

A shadowy light fell across Timbre Ann. It shone on the bluebird brooch pinned to her chest. Sam must've taken it off Henri for safekeeping; he must've given it back to Timbre Ann. Seeing it, my chest pained. I had so wanted to buy that brooch for Henri, but the moment I saw it on her chest at Biggs Repair, the blood oozing out under her breast, I'd realized it hadn't been my gift to give. Henri was Timbre Ann's kin, so it was right that it came from her. And my not being able to afford it didn't mean I loved Henri any less.

I set the sandwich plate on the bedside table. Even though I knew that Henri's body was being prepared at Johnson's funeral home for whatever went on in its crematorium, for a half a second, I could see her lying beside Timbre Ann on the bed, cradling her. I could see the outline of her hips, and the way she towered over Timbre

Ann. She turned her head over her shoulder, stretching out one arm to me.

Like always, and for my whole life, Henri led me, calling me forward.

The bed creaked as my knee hit the mattress. Timbre Ann didn't scooch forward to give me room, but she didn't stiffen. She was still taller than me, but I did my best to wrap my body around her. Once I put my arms around her, her shoulders shook. She shook so hard that the bed moved. It rose gently, up and down, as she cried. I rested my palm flat on her back and made circles, tracing the same patterns over and over, the way Henri had calmed Mama.

Neither one of us had Henri now. We only had each other.

"He's sorry," I said.

She turned to me, her face swollen and blotchy. "Who?" she asked.

I'd meant Peter, whose back shook the same as hers, but what I said was, "They both are. Peter and Daddy." In my heart, I knew it was true.

FIFTY-FIVE
Mount Zion

"Lisbeth, honey," Daddy said. He wore the same suit he'd worn to Meemaw's funeral, minus the blue handkerchief. He didn't look dapper; his face and ribs were bruised. "We should leave now."

He wrapped his knuckles softly on their bedroom door, then opened it, but Mama didn't come out. She sat on the corner of the bed, her hands clasped together, staring blankly out the window. The pine trees were still green, but the other trees—maples, oaks—their leaves were just beginning to yellow.

"Let me, Daddy," I said. "I'll get her."

He nodded. He'd kept his promise. He still hadn't taken a drop. It was long past sunrise when we got home. Daddy must've thought we weren't coming back. I wasn't sure if we were, either, but when Mama got in the truck, she drove us to the bank and then back home. Daddy sat at the kitchen table, staring at a bottle of whiskey. The seal hadn't been broken. "I'm so sorry, Lisbeth," he said, not hanging his head. He made not one excuse.

"Oh, Otis," Mama had said, her eyes so red-rimmed I bet she could barely see. "Sorry isn't going to bring her back, now is it?"

Daddy poured himself some strong black coffee. "No. No, it isn't," he said.

Now, I pushed open the bedroom door. It was time to go.

"Mama." I kneeled before her, patted her too-still hands. "We've got to go now. To say good-bye to Henri."

Before getting up, she kissed my forehead. "All right, sugar," she said. "I'm ready." In the thin hallway, she brushed past Daddy, not saying a word. I couldn't rightly say she was giving him the silent treatment. Since the fire, we'd all just fallen mute.

We climbed in the truck and not one of us looked back at our tiny pillbox house. Mama sat me in the middle, again between her and Daddy. My walking stick rested on the back of the seat, in the same spot where the Sheriff kept his rifle in his patrol car. I held a small suitcase on my lap. Inside, the baby blanket Mama had crocheted was wrapped around my nest, the one nest I had left. The other

I had already left in a special spot: Timbre Ann's and my willow.

We pulled into the Biggses' church, Mount Zion Missionary Baptist. The parking lot, a patch of dry Georgia clay, was already full, so Daddy had to angle the truck near a ditch far behind all the other cars. That was all the room there was. I reckoned Henri wasn't a second mother only to Mama. She'd made sure everyone she knew had a full belly and got more than their share of hugs.

Mama climbed out of the truck cab. She gave me her hand, helping me down, so I didn't hurt my ankle or muss my dress. It, too, was the same thing I wore to Meemaw's funeral, the green dress with the white islet flowers. I looked at my ankles, peeking out over the top of Timbre Ann's patent leathers. Sam had said, where there is a need, you fill it. I reckoned all the Biggses had seen the need in us Baxters.

"Look at all the people," Mama said. "Even more than the other night at Sam's."

Henri had been right. "I know my worth," she'd said once, when we'd been standing around Judge Anderson's kitchen. "When my day comes, the Lord above is going to welcome me with open arms." Surefire, all of Holcolm, colored Holcolm, was here to see her off.

Folks started to murmur when they saw us. They elbowed one another, whispered, and did all but point and say, "There, there, he was in on it. In on those fires. Yep, yep, he was."

My stomach turned flips. I hoped that we were welcome at the funeral. We weren't here out of disrespect. Not a one of us, even Daddy. He risked it all that night. Baxters' Gas-n-Sip would never open now. Not after Daddy had crossed both the Klan and the Council.

It was Mama who had decided. "We're moving," she'd said yesterday morning, when we returned home. "I've wired that interest money to another bank. One far away from here. We're taking our children and starting over somewhere safe." She wasn't worried about Daddy being pegged the patsy if Hoover's men, the FBI, ever did bother to investigate those fires. The night after Henri's death, we got our own death-threat brick through the window. The Sheriff was going to make us pay, one way or another. Leaving the Biggses, the only friends we had in Holcolm, had better be payment enough.

We made our way inside. Mount Zion looked nothing like Meemaw's church, with its fancy pillars, or like Trinity, with its worn hymnals.

"Let's sit here," Mama said. It was the second-to-last row.

Daddy nodded. The three of us took our seats. Mama kept her distance from Daddy. Unlike Meemaw's funeral, Daddy didn't pout. He didn't try to charm Mama or smile at her. Nothing. I reckoned he was just glad we hadn't left him, and he wasn't leaving us. A funeral was a stick-to-gether occasion.

I don't know why we had to pretend to squeeze in. There was plenty of room. The other folks in the pew, soon as they saw us, scooted away, treating us like the lepers that we were.

A voice behind me asked, "Were you at the fire?"

I turned to answer. "Yes, ma'am, I was."

The older woman patted my hand. "I thought so. My husband, my George, he told me how a white girl helped him, carrying him with the others. He's not here today, he still has that salve all over his burns, but I'm sure he'd want me to thank you."

"It was nothing, ma'am. Honest." That was the gospel truth. I should've helped sooner. Before the fires began, not after.

Music began to play—not organ music, but a piano. A jazz piano. Folks started humming and swaying. Mama, Daddy, and I sat with our backs rigid, feeling out of place. We didn't know how to move to the music. Clapping started. I thought of Henri singing in Sam's sedan, her head bouncing as she sang. For her I could give it a try. I clapped once, twice. I found the beat. Mama smiled a slow, soft smile. She picked up her too-still hands and began clapping, too. Daddy sat stock-still, but after a few bars, his leg moved, up, down, up, down, like he couldn't help himself. The music reminded me of the rain. The sure steady beat pinging on the roof of Daddy's truck.

"Excuse me?" Someone tapped Daddy on the shoulder. It was Peter. He wore a suit with a necktie. "Mr. Biggs would like y'all to move up front."

"Oh, we're fine right here," Mama said. She knew Peter was the one who shot Henri, who tried to shoot Daddy, but still she looked at him kindly. I did, too. Like Daddy, Peter had been trapped. Thinking that striking out—burning a building, or shooting a man—would make things better for the ones he loved. It didn't, for either of them. It only made things worse. Mama and Henri had been right: the fires hurt all of us, black and white.

"Well, I'm not supposed to take no for an answer," Peter stammered. I reckoned he was as nervous as all get out.

"Thank Mr. Biggs for the invitation," Daddy said. I could tell the invite made him uncomfortable. He rolled the funeral bulletin until it was so tight I thought it might disappear. "But we can't."

"Mr. Biggs said folks need it." This time Peter spoke calm and clear, making sure Daddy heard him good. "He said they need to see y'all sitting together. So folks stop talking, talking about revenge. That's what I did and look where it got us. We got to stop it now, before things get worse."

"He's right. That's true. Folks need it. I need it." I stood. I couldn't force Daddy, but I was done not doing the right thing, and not doing it at the right time. Either way, I was going.

"All right then." Daddy got to his feet. He winced, his ribs paining him. He held his hand out to Mama. And I don't know if it was the spirit of God's goodness floating through the cramped quarters of the church, but Mama took it.

Halfway up the aisle, Mama turned to see how I was doing, walking alone behind them, but I wasn't alone. I was with Peter. He had taken my arm and escorted me, as if he were taking me to a homecoming dance.

At the end of the aisle was my homecoming: Timbre Ann.

She waited, along with Sam, up at that very first pew. The family pew.

Sam nodded at us, his face taut with grief. Timbre Ann bit her lip and nodded, following her father's lead.

Peter went to sit with his family, and Timbre Ann's sad eyes followed him. She wasn't ready to forgive him or Daddy, and I could only hope that one day she'd forgive me.

Sam held out his hand. Daddy shook it. "We don't deserve this honor." Daddy's voice cracked.

"It's what Henri would've wanted," Sam said.

"Sit here, Polly." Timbre Ann moved the hymnal from the space to her left. There was a tinge to her voice—a "my pa is making me" tinge—but I didn't care. She was trying. We all were. And that, that was something.

Mama squeezed my arm. She linked her other arm with Daddy's and rested her hand on the growing swell of her belly. "Oh, Henri," I said. Tears came to my eyes. No numbers trick, not even Granddaddy's, would make it all right that my baby brother or sister would never know Henri. Wouldn't get to climb on her lap and tug at her hair. Wouldn't get to eat a slice of her coconut cake, or get a tongue-lashing for forgetting to wash before supper. It just wasn't fair.

One by one, people started rising. The music swelled, then stopped. The choir started humming the opening bars of "Amazing Grace." All around me, lips began to murmur. I didn't hum with them but closed my eyes and tried to breathe in the scent of the fresh lilies and the starched collars of the men's shirts. I felt all the folks standing behind us, behind Sam and Timbre Ann. All these fine folks would help Timbre Ann and Sam get up on their feet again. They'd make sure Biggs Repair got rebuilt. And what I left Timbre Ann at our special spot—at our willow—might help, too.

The humming was over. The singing started. I clutched the note I'd written early this morning.

Amazing Grace, how sweet the sound,
That saved a wretch like me.

I slipped the note into Timbre Ann's sweater pocket. She must've felt me do it. She went to open it.

"Later," I said, catching her eye. "Please, read it later." I couldn't stand the thought of her reading it here. Saying good-bye to Henri was hard enough.

"All right," she said, and put it back in her pocket.

As the strains of the music faded away, the preacher stepped to the pulpit. We sat. A hushed silence settled over us. I could feel it. All of us, that front pew, everyone there, we were ready to let the healing begin. We were ready to honor Henrietta Biggs.

"Brothers and sisters, sisters and brothers," the preacher said, his solemn voice filled with a great power. Timbre Ann slid her hand in mine. "Let us bow our heads and pray."

10/9/1959

Dear Timbre Ann,

We're leaving. Well, by the time you read this, we'll already be gone. I can't tell you where because I don't know yet. Mama said that when it's safe to write, I could. I'll address the letters in code, calling myself June Mason, from your favorite TV show and mine, so you know it's me. Otherwise, Miss Phelps at the post office might pull the envelope and show the Sheriff. We've got to think about things like that now, your family and mine.

Anyway, when I can write, I will. I hope you'll read my letters and write me back. Until then, I left you a reminder of me. Nope, not a school picture. A bird's nest. It's at our willow. You've got to go and get it. It was my first one—the one I used to start my collection. I found it in your backyard, so I reckon it was yours to begin with. I shouldn't have taken it without asking, but you had a ton of TLC from Henri and Sam, just like that baby bird had from its family, and I wanted it, too. I wanted it so bad I took that nest without asking. I am sorry for that. I am sorry for everything.

I know Sam got your money out—your college fund. I hope it's somewhere safe. We—Mama, Daddy, and I—

don't want him to have to touch a penny of your money to rebuild. So we left you something to help. It's nowhere near enough, but it's what we had to spare. So go and get the nest. You'll find the money there with it.

I'll miss you, Sam, and Henri.

> *Forever and always,*
> *Polly*

Author's Note

Polly and Timbre Ann's friendship is fictional. It is the exception—not the rule. During the Jim Crow and the Civil Rights Era, it was common for young black and white children to play together. But once they neared the teen years, these friendships were frowned upon or, as Sheriff Wilkes says to Polly about Timbre Ann, "Ain't you too old to be playing with the likes of her?" Yet such friendships probably existed despite the restrictions of segregation and society's attitudes, and girls with Polly's spunk and Timbre Ann's determination could have defied the odds.

In 1954, the US Supreme Court ruled in the landmark case of *Brown vs. the Board of Education*. This ruling outlawed racial segregation in schools and other public institutions because they violated the 14th Amendment to the U. S. Constitution. That meant that "separate but equal educational facilities" were finally seen for what they were: unjust and unequal. Because of this landmark ruling, there was an extreme reaction and resistance from many in the South. The Ku Klux Klan reacted harshly and stepped up the pace of lynchings, church burnings, and bombings that began during the Jim Crow era. Citizen's Councils formed widely in an effort to keep blacks and whites from being educated together. As a result, it took more than a decade for schools all over the South to integrate successfully.

Members of the black community also held meetings such as the one at Biggs Repair. Voter drives, protest planning, and non-violence training took place behind closed doors in an effort to organize the black community. These meetings inspired violence, often with the full knowledge and silent acquiescence of local law enforcement. Molotov cocktails, beatings, and fire hoses turned on protestors were only some of the tactics to keep African Americans from exercising their full rights as citizens. Many lost their lives—blacks and whites, the old and the young—in the struggle for freedom.

Acknowledgments

A book is built with more than words. It is built by belief — years of my belief and that of everyone I am lucky enough to have in my life. I offer a thousand thanks to:

My talented NYC writer's group: Laurie Calkhoven, Connie Kirk, and Josanne LaValley and our new addition, Kekla Magoon. Thank you for Thursday nights — the highlight of the week. I see your suggestions on every page. This book wouldn't be without y'all.

My Vermont College advisors: Norma Fox Mazer, Sharon Darrow, Marion Dane Bauer, and Tim Wynne-Jones, who gave me the tools with which to tell the truth. Thank you. With an additional heartfelt hug to Tim "Bear Hug" Wynne-Jones.

Alicia Potter, my VC chum, for asking the tough questions. If these characters are real, it is because of you.

John Menaker, for providing a safe space with plenty of Kleenex, and for helping me see the shades of gray.

My family: Allan Hegedus, Beth Hegedus, Susan Hegedus, Anna Mae Hegedus, Joseph and Marion Hegedus and Travis and Katie Simmons, who always called me the little engine that could, and finally I did! I take great pride in being a Hegedus and being an aunt to Allan, Emilie, Tehmin and Bella.

My New York City pals: including those who will always stay and those who have moved away, among them: Amy Botelho, Jonathan and Jennifer Forgash, David and Liz Riccerri, Annette Dator, Maggie Keller, Joe and DawnMarie Kerper, Zooey P., and Vernon Woolford, thank you for being my family of friends. With an additional "squeeze" to Amy and DawnMarie for their cheerleading and handholding.

Hollie Hunt, for having the courage on that hot summer day to tell me that I was a writer, not an actor. Our twenty-year friendship is part of the fabric of my life.

My first friends in Georgia: Amy Greeson and Kristy Milock. I couldn't have survived high school without you.

Dr. Fred Wharton, professor at Augusta State University, for asking: "Have you ever considered being an English major?" And all the teachers over the years who encouraged me.

To my students during the time I taught at Burke County High School in Waynesboro, Georgia. We only shared a year, but what a year it was.

Christina "Chrissi" Ross, my Southern vagabond friend, do not deny it; there are many books in you.

Richard Irving, for being a constant, "count-on-able" man. You entered after "The End" but I am glad you will always be my friend.

Additional Vermont College alums who offered insights: Sarah Aronson, Ed Briant, and Carrie Jones. Thank you for being my go-to readers. And to Sundee T. Frazier, for fielding my many emails.

To all of FD: especially Declan Kelly, Paul Keary, Brian Maddox, John Quinn, Gordon McCoun, Jennifer Doig, Sue Bloomberg, and Cathy Davis. Thank you for your continued support. It means more than you know.

My agent: Regina Brooks, for her enthusiasm and expertise.

My able publisher: Evelyn Fazio, for her passion and precision, and to all those at WestSide for their dedication and hard work.

I am grateful.